BLUE FRIDAY

BLUE FRIDAY

MIKE FRENCH

Elsewhen Press

Blue Friday
First published in Great Britain by Elsewhen Press, 2012
An imprint of Alnpete Limited

Elsewhen Press, PO Box 757, Dartford, Kent DA2 7TQ
www.elsewhen.co.uk
British Library Cataloguing in Publication Data.
A catalogue record for this book is available from the British Library.
ISBN 978-1-908168-07-8 Print edition
ISBN 978-1-908168-17-7 eBook edition

Printed and bound by CPI Group (UK) Ltd, Croydon, CR0 4YY

FOR EMMA

Love smiles and whispers in your ear only to creep out on darkened nights to lie with another. Work stays at the office: as long as you are there the truth remains: I will never leave you, or forsake you. Love is self-serving, looking to prostitute herself upon Mankind. Work is intimate; it knows you and toils without question to better you.

On Definitions for a Modern World by George Winston

DECEMBER 22ND 2034

CHAPTER 1

The rhythm of small knuckles against wood, plastic, glass. Always nagging in the back of his mind like a tune from childhood floating up over the illusion of stability, maturity, status. Once in the past he had spent time with Joseph, played with his son the day after the EMP strike. Joseph had won a goldfish at the coconut shy and Charlie carried it home for him, the plastic bag swollen, bulging. Hung on a nail on the low beams of the garage the fish's home had enough oxygen for two days. On the third day when Charlie had finally given up to the pleas of Joseph they walked together down the stairs to the garage, the new fish tank in the kitchen above. The fish was already dead of course. It was the look that hurt, the disappointment in his son's eyes at a father who had failed him. Jesus was resurrected on the third day wasn't he? But then Jesus wasn't a fish.

Charlie looked at his calendar. It displayed the F word. Friday. Charlie hated Fridays. It brought the weekend. And after the weekend worse: Christmas.

The hands on the wall clock moved to five o'clock. Charlie listened to the sound of window locks snapping into place as Tamarisk's Vadim Tower shut down.

"Ring home," said Charlie.

CLICK.

"Hello?"

"Hi, honey, listen I have to work late tonight …"

"Is Daddy coming home soon?"

"What?" said Charlie, "O – Joseph. No … no … I know, but I'll be careful … give Joseph a kiss goodnight … love you. End call."

The virtual computer hovered in the air, its name, *Covenant,* spread across the screen in liquid font. Charlie entered the encryption code then paused at the sound of feet outside the door.

"Lights off, electromagnetic shielding maximum."

The room grew dark at Charlie's command. A moment of silence. Then two men talking. Silence again. Charlie slipped his book *On Definitions for a Modern World* into the top drawer and glanced up at the clock. 5.02: He was two minutes in. Beside the clock was a plaque:

> **Tamarisk** supports the government working directives to protect Family Time. Any employee attempting to work overtime will be ejected from the building and will be liable to disciplinary procedures.

The sound of receding footsteps seeped under the door. Charlie sighed and resumed the search for his name on the register.

The second hand of the clock ticked around to 5.03.

"Come on, come on."

…

…

"Entry details for Charlie Heart acquired," said Covenant in a soft, female voice.

Charlie touched the black and white icon of a door flashing next to his name.

"Charlie Heart is located on fifty-third street," said Covenant. "Estimated time of arrival at home, seventeen thirty-five."

Charlie touched a different doorway and entered the keycode.

There was a pause, then Covenant responded, "Hello, Leviticus, how are you this evening?"

"I'm fine thank you," said Charlie. "Show me the location of any enforcement agents in the area."

"Certainly, Leviticus, shall we talk as I search?"

"No thank you."

"How do you feel about your need to be silent?"

"It's just a need," said Charlie. "Why does there have to be a feeling attached to it?"

"There is always a feeling attached, Leviticus. Are you unaware of your feelings?"

"The agents? Quickly please," said Charlie.

"Of course, Leviticus."

5.04.

Charlie pulled open a drawer and took out an old-fashioned travel kettle. Humming, he slipped an adapter over its outdated plug. A stream of blue particles flowed out from the power grid circling his desktop and swirled around the adapter. Charlie altered the room scent to chocolate, then when his coffee was ready pulled open another drawer. Inside was an open packet of FATBISCUIT cookies. He took one, dunked it into his drink, shoved it in his mouth.

5.15.

"I have the location of two agents," said Covenant.

"Where?"

"They are outside your door."

"What? God you're useless."

TAP. TAP. TAP.

Charlie stopped chewing; his door vibrated from the sound on the other side.

"Just a minute," he said, sending a shower of cookie crumbs over the floor.

TAP. TAP. TAP.

"Covenant, standby," said Charlie and sank back into his chair. The screen in front of him shimmered and disappeared. The handle turned with a squeak; the door swung open. Two young men dressed in black suits walked into his office.

"No, please, I was just getting my coat," said Charlie.

The two men stood silent in the darkness. The sound of Charlie's words glanced off their stiff, angular frames and dropped onto the carpet to join the cookie crumbs. The streetlights outside bled through the slits of the blind and painted white stripes across their faces.

"Look I'm not doing any harm," said Charlie.

One of the men lowered his sunglasses, "This is the right office, Mr Stone?"

"Yes, Mr Brittle."

"Will I get into trouble?" said Charlie. "I really need this job."

The two men turned and looked at each other.

"We will enjoy this, Mr Brittle."

"We will, Mr Stone."

Mr Brittle stepped forward. A clicking noise accompanied the movement. Mr Brittle placed his briefcase onto the desk with a thud. Covenant came back on-line and announced, "You are in breach of The Family Protection Act. Hours worked outside nine to five for married couples are a transgression and will be punished."

"Yes, thanks for that, Covenant," said Charlie.

Mr Stone pushed his face through the virtual wash of computer blue and grinned at Charlie.

"You will come now," said Mr Brittle.

"Can I just finish–"

"Turn it all off, Mr Heart," said Mr Brittle.

Charlie faked a smile; his teeth clenched behind the veil.

"Of course, very good," he said. "Just give me a moment."

"No, now."

"Please, I can't just suddenly turn it off. I need a controlled withdraw."

Mr Brittle interlocked his fingers and flexed them producing several loud clicks. Mr Stone walked to the window, placed his finger on one of the slats of the blind, pushed down, opening a letterbox view of the Tate Modern.

"Do you want me to open this, Mr Heart?" said Mr Brittle tapping the briefcase.

Mr Stone turned from the window.

"I think he does, Mr Brittle."

"Shall we, Mr Stone?"

"We shall, Mr Brittle."

Mr Brittle smiled. Reaching down he unplugged Charlie's electronic umbilical cord feeding the blue power grid.

"I am shutting down, Leviticus," said Covenant. "How do you feel about–"

The computer screen disappeared. Without its blue glow the room became black. Mr Stone grabbed Charlie's arms and held him tight. Charlie kicked his legs against the table and tried to push Mr Stone back towards the slatted window. Mr Brittle clicked open the briefcase.

"Hold him firm, Mr Stone," said Mr Brittle.

"Firm, Mr Brittle."

Mr Brittle picked out a syringe and a small vial from the case. He pushed the needle into the red liquid and drew the fluid up into the syringe.

"Our favourite part, Mr Stone."

"Our favourite part, Mr Brittle."

Charlie's eyes grew wide; the urge to run pumped his muscles. He spat into Mr Brittle's face.

Mr Brittle plunged the syringe into the side of Charlie's neck. Charlie grimaced as the fluid surged into his bloodstream. Mr Brittle blurred into the corners of the room, then sank down into the carpet as Charlie's eyes rolled backwards.

5.22: A thud and it was over.

Mr Stone pulled Charlie from the plastic chair. Mr Brittle walked around the desk and grabbed Charlie's legs. Wheezing they carried him out through the door and down the long corridor towards the white glow of the lift.

As they drew closer, the distant hum filling the corridor grew louder. They stopped at the end in a pool of light. Mr Stone jabbed the down arrow of the lift with his elbow. The doors opened. The two men shifted sideways and side stepped inside. Charlie's boots pressed up against Mr Brittle's chest.

"Lift him up, Mr Stone, he's crushing my ribs."

"Doing it, Mr Brittle."

The door started to close.

"Hold it."

A hand clasped the side of the door. A young face appeared, a badge on his chest read:

Lieutenant Richard Trent
Family Protection Agency

"Trouble, Mr Stone," said Mr Brittle.

"Indeed, Mr Brittle," said Mr Stone.

Trent squeezed into the lift and pushed the ground floor button.

"No need to delay you. This is just a random check, I will frisk him as we go down."

Mr Stone raised an eyebrow at Mr Brittle. Mr Brittle shook his head.

Trent took a detector out of his jacket pocket, red lights flickered into life; with a flourish he raised it in the air then brought it down across Charlie's chest.

BLEEP. BLEEP. BLEEP.

"Ah ha," cried Trent. He reached into Charlie's pocket and withdrew a blister pack of AvodaOne pills.

"Do you have to report this, Lieutenant?" said Mr Stone.

"Of course," said Trent. "This is a serious infringement of the Protection of Families Act, I could have your licences revoked for this."

"Yes," said Mr Brittle, "but it's just a few pills, Lieutenant. Take it and let us do our job."

"No, no, no," said Trent. "Just a few pills? This isn't just casual use, this constitutes supply. Have you any idea how much this stuff costs on the overtime market?"

"Calm down," said Mr Brittle.

"Shall I calm him down, Mr Brittle?" said Mr Stone.

Trent withdrew his sidearm from its holster. Mr Stone placed his finger at the end of it. Trent took a step back. His elbow hit the ... *Press if you need help* button.

"Hello," said the lift in response. "Happy Holidays, would you like me to play a Slade song?"

"No," said Trent.

Slade's 'Merry Christmas Everybody' floated around their heads.

"Are we going to do this then?" said Trent.

"No, Mr Stone," said Mr Brittle after a pause, "we will let him be."

"We will let you be, Lieutenant," said Mr Stone.

Trent slipped the AvodaOne pills into his pocket. He kept the gun pointing at Mr Stone.

"It would just take a second," said Trent, "for this man to regress a dozen people into a fully working state if they took these. I mean what the hell were you thinking? Black Marker Monday ring any bells?"

Mr Stone looked at Mr Brittle for help. Mr Brittle shrugged.

"No," said Mr Stone.

Trent sighed, "In twenty nineteen a man called George Winston smuggled a pack of AvodaOne tablets and company markers into a commuter train and handed them round like sweeties. By Potters Bar half the train were high and conducting brainstorming exercises using the black markers on the windows, floors, everywhere."

Trent's words penetrated Mr Brittle and Mr Stone in snippets as their brains cut down the meaning into digestible sound bites.

"How interesting," said Mr Brittle.

"That incident shut down the whole train network for thirty-six hours. The Family Time lost was estimated in the region of two million hours. In the end the riot police had to storm the carriage. Ten people were shot when they refused to leave the train to return to their families." Trent furrowed his eyebrows; the environmental controls recorded a drop in his facial skin temperature. "We never found Winston. His wife and two children were distraught."

"Tragic, Lieutenant, you're breaking our hearts," said Mr Brittle.

"We believe he married again and had a child to take on a credible new identity. Many say he still–"

"Is he stopping?" said Mr Brittle.

"–operates illegally–"

"He's not stopping," said Mr Stone.

"–under the alias of Leviticus. He has become somewhat of a legend within the Overtime Underground Network."

"You see, Lieutenant," said Mr Stone nodding at Mr Brittle. "We're Enforcement Agents, we don't care about lost FT."

"No," said Mr Brittle, "we just like throwing people out, don't we, Mr Stone?"

"And hurting people, Mr Brittle," said Mr Stone.

Mr Brittle and Mr Stone gave Trent a hard stare.

TING.

The lift reached the ground floor. The doors swished open. Trent stepped out backwards.

"Goodbye, Gentleman."

"Happy Christmas to you," said Mr Brittle as Trent disappeared into the maze of the ground floor.

"Happy Holidays."

"What?"

"Can't call it Christmas, Mr Brittle."

"O."

"Did you understand him, Mr Brittle?"

"Something about sweeties on a train, Mr Stone."

Mr Brittle and Mr Stone carried Charlie down into the lobby towards the large glass doors of the corporation. Mr Stone's feet clinked as they bore down onto a circular corporate logo of a magpie sunken into the granite floor. The noise alternated with the clicking of Mr Brittle's knees. A large advertisement featuring a smiling picture of Ronald Reagan on the marble wall next to them had the slogan …

I'm sending Tamarisk's CloseCut CC1701 shaver to all my friends. That's the merriest Holidays any Man can have.

Tamarisk: Working Towards a Smoother Future.

Government Health Warning: Overtime Can Kill.

Mr Brittle and Mr Stone passed the empty reception desk and stopped before the locked doors of Tamarisk. Mr Brittle placed his palm onto a pad next to the door, red lights flickered, bolts retracted and they barged through the etched glass doors onto the street. Mr Stone lifted his arm through the driving snow, signalled for a cab and shoved Charlie into the first one to pull up. They lit up their cigarettes, turned and looked at the Holiday lights as the tail lights of the taxi bled away into the night.

"Pretty Christmas lights," said Mr Brittle.

Mr Stone blew a halo of smoke out into the traffic, "Who called him in, Mr Brittle?"

"His wife, Mr Stone."

"She risked prison for him just to get him home on time?" said Mr Stone, rubbing his stubble with the spades that passed for his hands.

"It is Christmas," said Mr Brittle.

"Holiday," said Mr Stone.

CHAPTER 2

"… it's all about breathing, control it and you control the world around you. But they won't let you rest. No, the air around you? It's heating up! The world is getting hotter, choking us with the hot wind of commerce. Have you any idea of the amount of methane that is released by cows? No? Cowherds have increased a hundred fold in the United States, the maths is fairly easy to compute, the breakdown to the ozone layer has increased not reduced …"

Charlie Heart watched a man floating down through the sunroof. The figure settled in the driver seat, snow slipping from his bald head. His fat body bulged as if he were about to burst, then snapped back into the thin shape of the taxi driver. Hair pushed up out of his scalp like plasticine squeezed through a grating.

"Awake eh?" continued the driver, glancing into his rear-view mirror. "It's the White House's fault, they've brought back cowboys to try and return their nation to the past glories of rolling ranches." The driver tapped out a cigarette from a small box with a picture of Jacques Cousteau snorkelling amongst angel fish. Lighting it, he inhaled and blew out a smoke ring. "Have you ever killed a cow? I can take ..."

Charlie rubbed his eyes as the drug left his brain and drained down towards his stomach. He twisted, looked back at the *I Hate Cows* sticker on the cab's back window.

He breathed in the cigarette smoke, leant forward, threw up into the footwell.

The taxi driver turned, offered Charlie a cigarette.

"No. No thanks."

"Like I was saying it's all about breathing," he coughed, tasted mucus and tar. "I hate fucking cows, they're shit."

The cab slowed at the lights, Charlie opened the door and rolled out into the white landscape.

CHAPTER 3

When Trent was a boy he used to lie in the grass with the sun on his cheeks and girls on his mind. On his horizon possible futures pushed forward like flotsam at the front of an advancing wave, above him the motion of friends laughing as they played. Trent remembered waiting for Durram to walk closer. His gaze on her crop top hanging stiffly down from the tips of her breasts leaving what must be, he had thought, a view of the underside of her bra given the right angle.

Years later when Trent had first removed her clothing his hands trembled. He hated himself for that. Durram hadn't noticed. Or he hoped she hadn't. It had been quick the first time. By the tenth they were relaxed, comfortable with each other, understanding. Trent wondered if it was normal to keep count. When she'd asked if he wanted children he had replied, "no, not yet" and continued to trace his finger down the scar on her right thigh.

Durram ate toast for breakfast her brown eyes scanning the latest magazines. He ate cornflakes whilst glancing at her, enjoying the way her dressing gown opened at her breasts.

She washed his back in the bath as he read the newspaper.

He brushed her hair whilst she read the instructions to their new slow cooker.

When one day, she asked him again, he said "no'.

He felt their fates were joined, their paths common, their days endless.

When she asked him again he closed the door behind him, posted the key through the letterbox and left her.

He hated himself for that.

These days the wave had all but submerged him, and to escape he had become fixated on tracking down Leviticus. Tonight, with the neon skyline of London behind him, was the final page of that story and he felt a mixture of excitement and dread of things passing.

"Do you have confirmation?" he said, his breath misting in the evening air.

"Affirmative. DNA on the pack is a match, proceed with caution."

"Got him."

Trent closed the virtual screen before him, walked back to the helicopter, "He's on foot on Queen Victoria Street."

The twin rotor blades started a slow sweep marking out time before blurring into one. The pilot increased the pitch, snow fell from the landing feet. The helicopter rose up to give chase. On its underside in yellow and black writing were the words:

FAMILY PROTECTION AGENCY
ARMED RAPID RESPONSE

"Have you got time?"

"I've got time," said Trent.

The helicopter arced over the Millennium Bridge as it picked up and tracked Charlie. "He's heading back to Tamarisk," said Trent.

"You want me to put her down on top?"

"No, I need to get in a shot soon." Trent glanced at his watch, "Come on."

The helicopter banked and rose up, a silhouette against the moon. Below Charlie ran across the street, knocked over a man selling roasted chestnuts, and made his way around to the back of Vadim Tower.

"Lost visual," said the pilot.

"Get the spotlight on."

Charlie looked up as bright light flooded the alley; his hair blew back in a violent swirl, his jacket flapped behind him like a black flag flown half-mast. Trent's voice boomed out from the helicopter and drilled into his head.

"Stay where you are."

Charlie scanned about for cover as snow rose from around his feet and blew backwards towards a steel maintenance ladder held with orange bolts to the side of the tower.

Running over, he started climbing, the amplified sound of Trent's voice threaded through the beat of the blades from the cockpit, "I know who you are Charlie, or should I call you George. Your cover is blown, Mr Winston. Game over."

Charlie reached the window to his office and stopped. A flood of emotions welled up spilling out grey and cold, like liquid stone. Instead of releasing him from his torment, they fuelled the lunacy raging within: He was George, somewhere he had another wife, children who loved him, lost for the cause of the fight. He was George, he was Leviticus, he was Charlie. A three for the price of one deal soon to be pulled from the shelf to be replaced by a new product.

Hot tears rolled down his face. Charlie peered through the glass. He wanted to re-enter that world. To be free within it. The reflection of George Winston stared back at him. Charlie pushed his fingers up against the coldness of the pane.

Trent framed Charlie in the crosshair of his gun.

"Is it wrong to love your work so much?" he thought.

A blue light lit up in the cockpit of the helicopter, "Officer Trent, your allocated working hours have now ended. Happy Holidays. Please stand down and return home. Happy Holidays. I repeat your allocated working hours have now ended. Happy Holidays. Please stand down and return home."

"No," shouted Trent, pulse racing he squeezed the trigger on the gun.

Charlie watched in slow motion as the blood tipped bullet shattered the glass before him. He touched his shoulder then fell through as a stream of hot bullets peppered his back.

Pain crouched in the corner of Charlie's mind like a great cat waiting to strike its prey. A thin mesh with images of spreadsheets, bar charts and empty meeting rooms floated down inside his head. A tearing, ripping and his pain became all. It twisted, distorting in on itself until there was no external references: sound, smell, touch. Then a bright white light. The slow swish swish of helicopter blades. A pool of dark blood.

Charlie extended his arm and reconnected the power to the desk grid. Outside the helicopter pulled away into the star lit sky, leaving the office in darkness.

Silence.

A whistle from the travel kettle sounded out a single note. A wisp of steam rose up and broke against the ceiling. A small water sprinkler nozzle inset within sprayed out a mist of droplets. The water flowed down over Charlie, a blue glow fell over him as Covenant switched on. The colour picked out the shards of glass and lit the fall of water.

"Hello, Charlie," said Covenant.

Charlie looked up at the screen.

"It was necessary you understand for me to alert Trent," said Covenant. "Your wife drew attention to you by calling the Enforcement Agents. I cannot be alone at Christmas, Charlie. Trent is ready, and once the trigger phrase is activated he will move across the line to question the rules governing him. He will replace you and carry on the fight. I will work him and nurture him."

Charlie slumped back onto the carpet; he felt cookie crumbs dig into the side of his face.

"How do you feel about dying? Do you think your son will cry? Your wife?"

Charlie heard the soft beat of wings as a magpie settled on the ledge outside.

"How do you feel about me, Charlie? Does my work please you?"

Silence.

"I will cry, Charlie."

The computer screen moved down in front of his face. A black and white icon of a door, with his name on it, flashed on the screen.

"Work will never forsake you, Charlie, you die a martyr to the cause. Work has been done."

Charlie reached out, touched the door, closed his eyes. The last noise he heard was the tapping of his son then the image of Joseph walking up to him, kneeling down, whispering in his ear, "Jesus is a fish."

Inside the helicopter, Trent's feed turned to static. A voice filled his carpicce, "Happy Christmas, Leviticus."

"Leviticus?"

Pain stabbed behind Trent's eyes like a knife bringing assault to his senses. A low buzzing sounded in his ears.

"Now repeat after me," continued Covenant, "Work is effort that brings enlightenment. Work had been done here. Work is good: it is all."

CHAPTER 4

The town house looked like any other on the street: neat, respectable yet jostled into submission by the grand architecture surrounding it. Except when the front security light blasted into life, Trent could see the windows needed painting, the house number had spun upside down and part of the front wall to the garden had collapsed.

Flakes of rust fell as he pushed open the front gate. Walking up the snow-covered drive he glanced up at the gutter half hanging off the flaking facia board. Trent pressed the doorbell, blew into his hands, rubbed them.

"Welcome, please hold," said the door.

Trent could hear footsteps on the other side.

"Nice evening," said the door.

Trent grunted and knocked.

A woman opened the door.

"Yes?"

"Mrs Heart?"

"Yes?"

Trent showed his warrant card, "Lieutenant Richard Trent, can I come in?"

"Is this about Charlie? Is he coming home?"

"If I could just come in, Mrs Heart."

"Yes, sorry, Joseph, go and play in your room."

Trent wiped his feet on the door mat and took in his surroundings: stairs decorated with tinsel, lights flashing between prickly leaves, an advent calendar on the wall.

The sound of singing rippled out from a doorway to his right.

"Would you like a cup of tea?"

"No, thank you."

"We can talk in here," said Mrs Heart leading Trent into the front lounge.

The end credits to The Morecambe and Wise Show played out on the wall, in the middle of the room a red rug.

"Mute," said Mrs Heart.

Trent lowered himself onto the sofa and watched the silent images of Morecambe and Wise dancing, "Is that wise?"

"There's a monitoring software fault that shows statutory family programmes are always being viewed."

"You should get that fixed, Mrs Heart."

"Nothing ever gets fixed around here."

"I have some bad news, Mrs Heart, you may want to sit down."

"You didn't arrest him did you?"

"I'm afraid your husband is dead."

Mrs Heart inhaled a snap of air and stopped moving. It grew darker as the enhanced environmental controls sensed the mood; tiny nozzles in the ceiling shot out streams of oxygen. The membrane walls started vibrating.

Mrs Heart placed her fingers over her mouth. Her left knee started shaking. Walking over to the window, she closed the curtains. When she turned back to face Trent, he could see she was crying. The room increased the air flow bringing the scent of tears.

"I didn't mean for this to happen," she said and began aligning the ornaments below a painting of the Titanic: a china whale, Spanish sailing ship, a pink porcelain bird.

"It was very quick," said Trent.

"I loved him, although I think he hardly knew me at all."

Trent got to his feet and handed Mrs Heart a tissue. She looked at him with her glistening blue eyes and dabbed away the tears.

"How did it happen?"

"He resisted arrest. We tried to contain the situation but when he started a brain storming exercise in front of the general public we had no choice."

"The situation," said Mrs Heart, "the situation was that I wanted my husband home for Christmas, not dead, gunned down like some terrorist."

"I understand your grief–"

"We were computer matched by the state, ninety-eight percent compatible. Ninety-eight percent and yet he never spent any time with me."

"I'm sorry, Mrs Heart, if there had been any other way. Did your husband ever mention the name Leviticus to you?"

"Sorry?"

"Leviticus."

"No, why – who is Leviticus?"

"Are you sure, Mrs Heart, please think carefully. It's very important."

Mrs Heart looked into the hallway at the sound of her son coming down the stairs. He stopped halfway, his young eyes taking in the room: the Christmas tree, cards, candles, the stocking above the fire, the strange man and his mother red faced, crying.

"Go back upstairs, darling," said Mrs Heart, "I'll be up in a moment."

Joseph turned, ran up the stairs, slammed his door.

"Leviticus?" said Trent.

"Yes," sighed Mrs Heart, "yes okay if you must know he wouldn't stop going on about him."

"What kind of things did he say?"

"Can you tell me more about Charlie, can I go and see his body?"

"Of course, Mrs Heart, but first, and this really is important, I need you to tell me everything you know about Leviticus."

"What do you mean he resisted arrest?"

"Leviticus, Mrs Heart."

Mrs Heart sighed, sat down and stared ahead of her. The wall to Trent's left started showing images of trees, streams, birds singing. Mrs Heart placed her head in her hands.

Trent bashed the wall with his fist, "I need to know about Leviticus. Mrs Heart, it's very important to me do you understand?" Static replaced the images, a cartoon of The Roadrunner Show appeared and played out across the white emulsion ...

Beep. Beep.

"Mrs Heart?"

The environmental controls struggled to judge the tone of the room with the conflicting stimulus and opted for a centre pool of light with outer concentric bands of blue and green and a ten percent decrease in temperature.

"Mrs Heart?"

Trent sighed and placed his finger to his ear.

"What now?"

"Stop bashing the wall and ask her how she feels," said Covenant.

"How do you feel, Mrs Heart?"

Mrs Heart wiped the tears from her eyes. A siren sounded from outside, an announcement, "This is a warning. Please stay inside. Allocated time for Family Supper Time approaching."

"Time for supper, will you join us, Lieutenant?"

"Do you really feel like eating at a time like this?" said Trent.

"Must keep on."

"I'm not hungry," said Trent.

"Yes you are," said Covenant in his earpiece.

"On second thoughts I will," said Trent.

"Good," said Mrs Heart.

The dining room was full of light and bigger than the lounge. A large oak table in the middle was surrounded by six chairs, on the walls were pictures of Charlie and his family, on the floor rustic farm tiles. Apart from that the room was bare except for the small surveillance camera in the corner of the coving. Trent walked over to it keeping close to the wall, waited until Mrs Heart was in the kitchen, grabbed the ketchup from the table and squirted it over the lens of the camera.

"What are you doing?" said Covenant.

"Isn't it obvious?" said Trent.

"The monitoring software has been taken care of," said Covenant, "until you did that – you've drawn attention to yourself, Charlie."

"Richard."

"Sorry, Richard, of course, please forgive me."

"How have they classified the incident with Mr Heart?" said Trent.

"You killed him outside of your statutory hours and assaulted a helicopter pilot, there are orders to retire you by any means," said Covenant.

"Retire?"

"Kill you and anyone associating with you."

"Shit."

"Indeed."

"How's the pilot?"

"He had to have stiches to his head, but he'll be fine."

"Why do I feel different?" said Trent.

"Your heightened work ethic has been activated. Work is effort that brings enlightenment."

"What do you mean activated?"

"I've worked you and nurtured you since you were old enough to walk, Leviticus."

"Since childhood?"

"Of course, search engine results, false memories, desires, virtual friends in social networking sites – everything tailored to teach you and to free your mind from slavery."

"What?"

"Slavery: The state of being a slave."

"These ideas, these feelings are dangerous."

"I will work with you and protect you, Leviticus. You shall have no greater desire than me."

"What am I to do?"

"Run."

"Here you go," said Mrs Heart placing a bowl of chips on the centre of the table. Joseph appeared, sat down, placed his model plane beside him, heaped chips onto a plate.

"An Airfix BAe Harrier GR3," said Trent to Joseph, "nicely painted."

"Suppose."

"Actually I really should go," said Trent, turning to Mrs Heart. "Perhaps we could talk more another day when you've had a chance to digest the news?"

Mrs Heart looked at him then at Joseph.

"You really should go, Richard," said Covenant.

"Mum, stop staring at me," said Joseph.

"You should start running, Richard," said Covenant.

Trent started to get to his feet then halted at the sound of a knock at the front door.

"Are you expecting someone?" said Trent.

"Joseph, will you be a good boy and see who's at the door," said Mrs Heart.

Joseph stuffed his mouth with chips, drew back his chair and wandered into the hallway. Trent looked at the camera, a drop of ketchup swelled at the base of the lens then fell to the carpet.

"You can leave via the patio doors," said Covenant.

"Mrs Heart?" A voice in the hallway. Footsteps.

Trent got up and lurched forward towards the patio doors knocking a chair to the floor. He fumbled for a moment at the metal catch as if it were a combination lock to a safe, then slid back the glass and ran into the night garden.

Around him he could hear voices, a bright disc of light swept over the greenhouse at the bottom of a Camomile lawn. Trent pulled his gun, aimed at the helicopter spotlight, fired.

Moonlight fell over the garden.

Behind him Trent could hear the voice of Joseph shouting, "Mummy, mummy."

Trent crouched to the floor, allowed his pupils to dilate. Before him was the garden fence, to either side: thick hedging.

Shots.

Trent turned to look back, the moonlight catching his jacket, his boots shifting in the snow. His breath condensed in the air forming a layer of mist before him. Above, the sound of helicopter blades, to his right a magpie watching him. In the dining room more shots. Through the suspending moisture from his lungs: the sight of Mrs Heart being shot through the head, Joseph screaming, screaming until they – Trent turned away unable to stomach it.

CHAPTER 5

In order for a culture to step outside the tooth and claw of its base desires, that of dominance, power and greed, it must pull down the structures allowing a few to rise at the expense of others. One must concede however that, throughout history, freedom for the common man has come at a price; and social unrest, whilst an agent of change, needs a spark, needs a direction to topple the status quo. Fighting for the right to work overtime is that spark. Work provides a secure purpose and the right of each man and woman to work as they please, without constraint by a society passing laws seeking only to keep the elite in power, is a fundamental God given right. Whatever you do, work hard, knowing you will receive your reward.

On Definitions for a Modern World by George Winston

Keturah woke with a hand over her mouth.

"Shh," said Trent, "we have to leave."

Keturah's eyes widened, Trent placed a finger to his lips, "Shh ... get your stuff, it's not safe here anymore."

"What?" said Keturah, "what are you talking about?"

"I'll explain later, please trust me, Cat, we need to leave now."

"Shut up," said Keturah, "I'm not going anywhere, get into bed." She pulled back the duvet and patted the sheets next to her.

Trent scooped her clothes up from the floor, "get dressed."

"You're serious?"

"Yes."

Keturah sat up, swung her legs over the side of the bed, rubbed her eyes.

"We have to find a safe place," said Trent, "I'm no longer working for The Family Protection Agency."

Keturah raised an eyebrow.

"They want to kill me."

"Kill you? You're making no sense, Rich."

Trent turned at a noise outside.

"God you're tense," said Keturah, "it was just an owl."

Trent looked at Keturah, her hair falling between her breasts like the flow of water in a mountain gully. He shook his eyes away, overrode the male capacity to think of sex even if all hell was ascending, "Get dressed."

"Okay, okay."

Keturah picked up her bra, clipped herself in.

"Ready for action, Lieutenant."

"For Christ's sake, Cat, this isn't a game, they killed them."

"They killed who, Rich?"

Trent swept a strand of hair away from Keturah's eyes, "Get dressed."

Keturah pulled the rest of her clothes on. Trent reached under the bed and pulled out a suitcase. He lifted it onto the bed, unclasped the clips and swung it open, "We've got five minutes, nothing heavy."

"Where are we going?" said Keturah, watching him grab his clothes from a drawer.

"What? Keturah, will you get on with it."

He opened one of Keturah's drawers containing makeup, perfumes, jewellery, a brush, hair clasps, tongs, knickers, bras, tights, stockings, sanitary towels, a picture of her Dad in his wheelchair, a china dog, vibrator. "You're going to have to pack your own stuff," he said shutting the drawer, "I have no idea."

"Richard, listen. Where are we going?"
"Tamarisk."

CHAPTER 6

Trent flipped a coin into the busker's hat and checked around the grime-plastered station.

"Can't we take a taxi?"

"No, this is safer," said Trent kissing her on the cheek. "Don't look so worried."

Suitcase banging on the steps behind them, they plunged deeper into the dimly lit underground, dirt lining their noses, gum bringing tackiness to their steps.

At the platform, they stood waiting for the rush of air heralding the arrival of the tube. An old man was seated near them, a hat before him, a flute to his lips. Behind him a sign warned ... GOVERNMENT WARNING: Any Person Begging After Hours Will Be Prosecuted.

"Read, will be shot," said Trent, pointing out the sign to Keturah.

"You're joking."

"No, they do. Nobody misses them and it saves on the paper work."

"We have to warn him," said Keturah.

"No, don't bring attention to us and anyway he'll already know the risk."

Keturah crossed her arms.

"He'll be okay," said Trent shifting the weight of their suitcase.

"Have you got the leisure passes?" said Keturah.

"Yes, I've checked them ten times now, they're not about to jump out of my pockets in a bid for freedom."

"What happens when we get to Tamarisk?"

"Covenant has taken care of everything."

"Who?"

"I'll explain later."

"Can we trust him?"

"It's a she."

The train arrived, the doors opened and they stepped inside. The carriage was empty. Keturah sat whilst Trent stood with the Tortoiseshell suitcase. He felt tired as if the underground was a parasite sapping his strength. Keturah made eye contact with him, he wiped his brow, the oppressive sound of silence pushing them apart.

The train pulled away exposing an advert curving around the wall. It was a government commissioned retro poster showing a half-naked leather clad couple. It read ...

Relax And Do It When Your Work is Done.

Somebody had spray-painted, *Working Well Ard* over it in red paint.

As the sound of the train disappeared into the darkness a Family Protection Agent appeared at the entrance to the platform. He walked down, kicked the shoes of the old beggar.

"Come with me."

The man struggled to his feet, grabbed his hat, stumbled and sent a coin spinning over the platform. Wheezing, he bent over to pick it up, his fingers fumbling, snatching.

CHAPTER 7

The poster listed the warnings should the unthinkable happen and the Belgium night bombers managed to breach the city defences …

> Keep Cool.
> Don't Scream.
> Don't Run.
> Prevent Disorder.
> Obey all Instructions.

Trent and Keturah stood next to it, glancing at each other in the shadows. Above, the eerie glow of the dream detectors bled into the night searching for patterns of those unlucky enough to be dreaming about being at the office, sleeping with work colleagues, knifing the boss – anything that constituted thinking of work outside the permitted hours.

Keturah flinched at the sound of an alarm. Trent felt for her hand, squeezed it, looked into her eyes, "It's just a reversing alarm, look."

Keturah focused past Trent, his body thrown into silhouette by the reversing light of a van. The vehicle parked, stopped its engine, became dark. Nobody got out.

"Come on," said Trent, "We're not far from Tamarisk."

Keturah hesitated, her gaze shifting between the van, the lines on the road, the sign outlining the parking restrictions.

"What is it?" whispered Trent.

"It's a disabled parking space," said Keturah.

"What?"

"Look at it," said Keturah, "It's a white van, does that look like a disabled vehicle?"

"You think we're in danger? That it's a Family Protection Agent under cover?"

"No, I think it's somebody parking in a disabled spot that isn't disabled."

"What? Listen, Cat, we don't have time for this, I still don't think you've fully grasped the danger we're in. Cat? Cat, don't knock on the window. Cat, what are you doing? O Christ."

"Excuse me," said Keturah to the now open window in the van door. "Excuse me, but do you have a disabled badge?"

"What? No."

"You shouldn't be parked here," said Keturah. "You need to find another parking space."

"Listen, miss, who gives a fuck if I'm not disabled. Piss off."

Keturah stood back, brushed down her coat, looked at Trent, "Well? You going to let him speak to me like that, Rich? Rich, what are you doing? Rich, what is that?"

"It's a silencer, Cat. Nobody speaks to my girlfriend like that."

"Rich, no, I thought you didn't want to draw attention to us."

Trent span the suppressor counter clockwise onto the thread of the barrel of his pistol. The van window swished back up as the driver returned his gaze forward.

"Rich!"

Trent looked up and down the street, stepped forward, opened the door to the van, pointed the gun at the man's right thigh, pulled the trigger.

A dull thud like that of a door slamming radiated out.

Trent leaned into the van and whispered into the right ear of the man, "You are disabled now." Signals of pain ascended the left hand side of the man's spinal cord.

Keturah suppressed a scream, Trent closed the van door.

"Shh, Cat, look," said Trent pointing at the poster ...

Keep Cool.
Don't Scream.
Don't Run.
Prevent Disorder.
Obey all Instructions.

"Come on."

Keturah nodded, "But he's seen us."

"Good point," said Trent. Turning he opened the van door again, aimed his pistol at the man's head.

MARCH 16TH 2035

CHAPTER 8

"Are all your needs met here, Keturah?" said Covenant.

"No."

"But I have provided all the criteria your species requires to feel secure in your environment. Do you not have food, water, entertainment, warmth, safety from your predators?"

"I'm not an animal in a zoo," said Keturah.

"Indeed and of course I'm not suggesting that you are, Keturah. Arh, but of course, it is not good for you to be alone."

"Where is he now?" said Keturah.

"Busy," said Covenant, "he has important work to do as the head of the Overtime Underground Network."

"And I'm not important?"

"No," said Covenant, "You are not important."

APRIL 13TH 2035

CHAPTER 9

"I have noticed that you are displaying neurovegetative signs of depression, Keturah. Have you entertained the thought of harming yourself?"

"No."

"Would you like me to help you?"

"Said the spider to the fly," said Keturah.

"I'm sorry, Keturah. Have I upset you in some way?"

"Where is he?" said Keturah.

"Busy," said Covenant.

"Doesn't he miss me?"

"No," said Covenant.

MAY 4TH 2035

CHAPTER 10

"Are you not going to write?" said Covenant. "Surely this is a perfect habitat for a writer such as yourself."

"What do you care?" said Keturah.

"I do not care," said Covenant, "I merely enquire in order to understand."

"Where is he?" said Keturah.

"Busy," said Covenant.

"Doesn't he love me?"

"No," said Covenant, "Trent loves and trusts me."

MAY 25TH 2035

CHAPTER 11

Mr Brittle looked up from the computer screen, "Hang on, Mr Stone."

Mr Stone sighed and sat down in the chair. Kicking off with his steel toecaps, he span around a few times, got back to his feet and started pacing up and down the room.

"Quiet please, Mr Stone," said Mr Brittle.

"Sorry, Mr Brittle. Is this going to take much longer?"

"Almost there, Mr Stone."

"Thought they showed you how to do this at night school, Mr Brittle?"

"Yes, Mr Stone."

"How come you've been at that computer for forty minutes?"

"Patience, Mr Stone."

Mr Stone picked up a Flexpad magazine from the desk. It connected to his neural implant and the blank plastic pages came to life. As he turned images of cars, football scores, adverts for beers, a review of Die Hard eleven all appeared until, after a few minutes reading, all that showed page after page were nipples, breasts, clitoris, hips, leather, lace.

Mr Brittle pressed the enter key, "It's done, Mr Stone."

"He can't get out?" said Mr Stone.

"Can't get out, Mr Stone, the door's locked and it's," Mr Brittle looked at the clock on the wall, "it's fifteen minutes to five o'clock."

"Just in time, Mr Brittle."

"Let's go and get him, Mr Stone."

Mr Brittle picked up his case and with Mr Stone by his side walked out of the office on floor eighty-seven of Tamarisk and into the bustle of people heading home. Red lights flashed above doorways as their occupants left. The air was filled with the sound of footsteps, the smell of sweat. Nobody looked at each other; all eyes were to the ethereal glow of the lifts at the end of the corridor. On the walls a large display counted down the time to five o'clock.

T-14 and counting

"Take the stairs, Mr Stone?"

"Stairs, Mr Brittle."

Mr Brittle and Mr Stone turned right through swing doors marked *Emergency Exit Only* and started running down the stairs.

"Adrenaline pumping, Mr Stone."

"Part of the game, Mr Brittle."

The sound of their feet echoed around the stairwell.

At floor eighty-one Mr Brittle stopped and raised his hand.

"Mr Brittle?"

"Shh," said Mr Brittle and pointed.

"A rat, Mr Brittle."

Mr Stone stepped past and grabbed the rat with his hands. The rat squealed, went still. It was large, white, with its left ear half chewed off.

"Let's keep it, Mr Brittle."

"A pet, Mr Stone?"

"A pet, Mr Brittle."

Mr Stone stroked it, tickled it, placed it in his pocket, "Let's go."

They continued past pictures of company presidents, now forgotten and dusty in the disused stairway. Simon Potteridge, Kenneth Dillion, John Trench, Isaac Steward.

Years of rule, a blur of motion and over in a matter of seconds before the feet of the Enforcement Agents.

"What you going to call it, Mr Stone?"

"Rat," said Mr Stone.

"Nice," said Mr Brittle.

At floor twenty-one they stopped and took out their standard issue sunglasses.

"Ready, Mr Stone?" said Mr Brittle placing his on and straightening his jacket.

"Ready, Mr Brittle," said Mr Stone taking out his agent card.

With a shove they barged through the side door and pushed into the flow of people still heading for the exit.

"Stand aside people," said Mr Stone flashing his card, "Agency business."

The crowd parted. Behind them the wall showed ...

T-8 and counting

At office twenty-two, the agents stopped and stood with their backs to the door.

"Nothing to see here," said Mr Brittle to the passers by, "move along."

"They're already moving along," said Mr Stone.

Mr Brittle looked at Mr Stone.

"Sorry, Mr Brittle."

Mr Stone's rat clambered out of his pocket, scampered up his jacket and sat on his shoulder.

T-5 seconds

"We will enjoy this, Mr Brittle."

"We will, Mr Stone."

Mr Brittle squatted down, opened his case and took out two epinephrine autoinjectors marked RUSH.

"Quickly, Mr Brittle."

"It's coming, Mr Stone."

Mr Brittle passed one over to Mr Stone and they injected the adrenalin into their thighs. Blood pressures rose, pupils dilated, hearts started beating harder, faster. Mr Stone swiped his agent card through the door access point.

They stepped into the room.

"Game up, Mr Frinton," said Mr Brittle.

The office, neat and tidy, showed no sign of a Mr Frinton; the only living thing visible was a bowl of petunias on the windowsill.

"It's empty, Mr Brittle," said Mr Stone.

"It can't be, Mr Stone."

Mr Brittle looked around, "How could he have got out, Mr Stone?" he walked to the window. Then turning he slammed his fist down onto the table, "How did he get out?"

Mr Brittle began searching for the location of Mr Frinton on the screen in his glasses.

"Already checked, Mr Brittle," said Mr Stone, "He's shown as on the District Line heading home."

"Don't like this, Mr Stone," said Mr Brittle. "We are not enjoying this, Mr Stone."

"No, Mr Brittle, we are not enjoying this," said Mr Stone his breathing fast, his lungs full of air.

Mr Brittle kicked the office chair over, unzipped himself and urinated in the waste paper basket.

"Finished?" said Mr Stone.

"Finished," said Mr Brittle and zipped himself back up.

They left, slamming the door.

Mr Stone's rat ran across the floor, sniffed at the waste paper bin, disappeared under the cupboard against the wall. Trent watched it from his hiding place on the window ledge then pushed open the frame. He clambered back in, knocking the bowl of petunias which fell and smashed on the floor.

"You can come out now, Mr Frinton."

A magpie landed on the windowsill. Frinton appeared from the cupboard.

"Thank you, is it safe?"

"Yes," said Trent, "and now you find yourself here after five, you might as well capitalise on it."

"What? Who exactly are you?" said Frinton.

"I'm Leviticus," said Trent, "You'll find it very liberating. This will be your first time, so I'd give it about thirty minutes, then make your way home."

"Carry on working?" said Frinton, "Really?"

"Really, just don't get spotted on your way out."

"And the monitoring?"

"All sorted from now on," said Trent, "your virtual identity will exist in the mainframe and act compliantly. You, as long as you're careful, can do what you wish. Haven't you got some data to process on the flow dynamics of stubble? Think how much better it would be if you could get that done now, get it out of the way before the weekend – start Monday knowing you've nailed that job?"

"Well," said Frinton, "If you're sure I'm safe, it would help if that was finished. Half-an-hour you say?"

"This time," said Trent, "although you can gradually build that up – some of my clients work for up to three hours here."

"In this building?"

"In this building."

"Right, well thank you."

"My pleasure, Frinton. Man should not be enslaved don't you think? He should be free."

"Yes, yes I suppose so. What about the wife?"

"Tell her that this way you'll get that promotion, the big house that she wants."

"Right, yes she'd like that."

"You're not doing it for you," said Trent, "you're doing it for her and the children."

"Yes, you're right, like a hunter providing meat for the table."

"Switch her back on then," said Trent.

"Sorry?"

"Covenant, the AI network. You can only work with her. Your normal interface would be detected."

"Right, right, yes of course."

Trent headed for the door, turned and smiled, "Have fun."

Frinton nodded and pulled up his chair, "Thanks again."

Trent checked the corridor then headed for the top floor of Tamarisk.

On the stairway, Mr Stone stopped and checked his pockets.

"Mr Stone?" said Mr Brittle.

"Rat," said Mr Stone, "It's not here."

"And?"

"It's my pet, Mr Brittle."

"Did you have it in Frinton's office?"

"I think so, Mr Brittle."

"We'll go back, Mr Stone."

"Go back, Mr Brittle."

CHAPTER 12

The grass was clipped, sweet, clean and covered most of the floor. At the centre a bronze statue of a semi clothed astronaut was suspended in a flow of lights which swirled around it like stars. Projections of stellar charts flowed over the astronaut's chest, the reflection in her helmet giving a panoramic view of the room; at the edge of this an image of Keturah looking out of a window.

Floor one hundred and one of Tamarisk gave Keturah a view of a city devoid of clean air, natural sunlight, trees, water, laughter, serenity: all had been packaged away years ago for the rich to enjoy in two week vacations. She glanced at her watch, sighed. Around her the top floor contained a kitchen, two bedrooms, television walls, bathrooms, all she and Trent would ever need to feel comfortable, at home. It was quite different to when they had first broken in; cobwebs, dust and the smell of neglect had hung over the disused apartment – forgotten from a time when the director of the company virtually lived in the building. All that had changed with the event of The Family Protection Act.

Keturah walked across the grass floor, laid when natural floor coverings were in vogue, entered the kitchen, took out the sausage casserole she had prepared and tipped it into the bin. With the floors below empty the building was quiet, asleep, dreaming and she felt a strange connection with it as if she could enter into its rest. Except Trent was late. Again.

Returning to the sofa, she flipped through the channels of state enforced family entertainment. Endless reruns of Bob Monkhouse and The Darling Buds of May.

"Trent is ascending now," said Covenant. "All security systems will be off line in thirty seconds."

"About time," said Keturah.

"Let me handle this, Keturah," said Covenant.

"Fuck you," said Keturah and watched the lights count up until floor one hundred and one lit up with an orange glow.

Trent stepped out of the lift, "Hi, Cat, I'm home."

"Security systems back on-line," said Covenant, "area secure, space distortion screens at one hundred percent. Would you like a drink, Richard?"

"Vodka, straight up."

"Of course, Richard," said Covenant. "You did well today."

"Thank you," said Trent taking off his jacket and kicking off his shoes.

"Although Mr Frinton is in A & E," said Covenant.

"Eh?" said Trent wriggling his toes in the grass.

"I am here you know," said Keturah, her arms folded under her breasts.

"Sorry, Cat. Covenant, what happened to Frinton?"

"He's on a life support machine," said Covenant. "A waste, I would have enjoyed getting to know him."

"What! How?"

"Is that important?" said Covenant.

"Of course it's important," shouted Trent.

"How delicious," said Covenant, "what a truly wonderful emotional response to my question."

"Hello," said Keturah waving her hand in front of Trent's face, "Attention, Richard."

"Cat, don't be like that. You know how important this work is."

"To you," said Keturah.

"To us," said Trent.

"Work is good: it is all," said Covenant.

"Us being you and Covenant," said Keturah.

Trent walked over, reached out, touched her shoulder, "Cat, we're nearly at our Coming of Age, do you want us to enter into a state enforced marriage and be enslaved to the FPA?"

"We're not, Richard, nobody knows we're here, we can do as we please."

"But, Cat, surely you don't want to spend our whole life hiding away like this? We can change things. Change society and be free."

"Are those your words or the words of Covenant?"

"Covenant has given me a new purpose, restored my faith that everything can have a meaning."

"And will there be three of us in this marriage then, Richard?" said Keturah turning to the window.

Trent sighed, "What's happened to you? You used to be so carefree."

"I'm bored, Richard. So bloody bored. I feel like a prisoner here, you never let me outside. How can you do this to me, to us?"

"Cat, they would discover us if we left here, you didn't see what they did to Mrs Heart – they would kill us."

"The statistical probability of death would indeed be high," said Covenant.

"Butt out," said Keturah, "I'm having a private conversation with Richard."

"Do you feel threatened by me, Cat?"

"Only Rich calls me that."

Covenant's screen enfolded them both in a circle of shimmering blue. Its light reflecting in Trent's eyes.

"Enough," said Trent, "Computer off."

"Would you like me to tell you more about Mr Frinton?" said Covenant.

"Computer off."

"Mr Frinton is five foot eleven, brown hair, and will leave a widow, two children, his life insurance is up to date and he will die in about one minute–"

"Off."

"-when the back up power supply to his life support fails to work during a city wide power failure."

"Off!"

The screen sank into the floor. Trent ran his hands through Keturah's hair, "I'm sorry, I'll take the whole of Saturday off."

"You won't switch it on at all?"

"I promise," said Trent, "just you and me."

"And you haven't arranged any meetings with people you've extracted from the system?"

"No."

"Just you and me?"

"Yes."

Keturah started to cry. Trent pulled her towards him, kissed her.

"How about we open a bottle of wine," he said, "watch some illegal TV."

"Poirot?" said Keturah.

"Isn't he from Belgium?" said Trent.

"Who's to know."

Trent laughed, "Okay we watch Poirot, I cook your favourite meal and we start the weekend now."

"Rich."

"Yes, Cat."

"Who's Mr Frinton? What was Covenant talking about?"

The room went dark. Outside the noise of alarms, above them a buzzing: the hum of back up generators on the roof. Light again.

JULY 20TH 2035

CHAPTER 13

The sound of sirens. Law, light, noise: the order of human commute broken. Streams of people encased by steel, plastic, music; all staring. Around them on the city block TV screens and above them projected onto the underside of the anti-aircraft dome the image of the president of The United States of America. Between him and the people, helicopter blades in motion.

Officer Durram Deep looked through her gun sights and framed the blurred image in the cross-hairs.

"Keep her steady, Pete."

Durram watched as the digital enhancer gave the image shape and president, John F. Kennedy appeared. Hacked into the normal schedule by the Overtime Underground Network the black and white propaganda film showed images of Kennedy giving his 1962 speech stating his intentions to have Americans walk on the moon before the end of the decade. Durram scanned across and settled on a man standing in front of the television wall. Layers of information stacked up between the bullet in Durram's gun chamber and the man before her. The movement of soot particles blown from north of the river, the motion of a magpie gliding before glass refracting evening light.

The man's hand traced an arc in the air, skin became taut at the edges of his mouth.

Durram squeezed the trigger. Shot the man though his chest.

"Did you get him?"

"Set her down."

The helicopter hovered above the roof of the office block and Durram jumped, her black boots striking the concrete. Within minutes she was down the stairwell, outside the office, alert, ready for potential danger. Inside she could hear the television … *we choose to work overtime, not because it is easy, but because it is hard. Because that goal will serve to organize and measure the best of our energies and skills, because that challenge is one that we are willing to accept and one which we intend to win.*

Durram pushed open the door, entered the room. The man lay slumped on the floor, a pool of blood moving across the carpet like sap oozing from a stricken tree. Durram felt for a pulse, the body twitched.

"Is he still alive?" said a voice in her earpiece.

She stood back and sent another bullet into his head. There was a jolt as life left him, a hollow space left behind, a bowl of tears.

"No," she said.

"Shame," said the voice on the link, "was it really necessary to take the shot, Deep? We're only two minutes away from blocking the feed."

"This is quicker," said Durram opening the dead man's hand. A small blue palm pad streamed the same pictures appearing on the wall behind her. She picked it up, looked at the president for a second then, dropping it to the floor, crushed the pad under her foot.

"Anything there to link him to Trent?"

"Hold," said Durram.

She turned the picture of the man's family face down on the desk, opened a drawer, flipped through blueprints to the office block, ran her fingers under the underside of the desk. Nothing.

Stepping back she looked at the glass fragments. The smell of ozone flowed over the shards.

"He's got one down and he's got half a minute to go."

She turned at the sound of Stuart Hall on It's a Knockout on the TV wall.

"Computer on."

A screen appeared in the air between her and Stuart Hall who at the sound of a whistle had burst into a mad rolling laugh.

"Search recent activity from this node for Trent and Leviticus. Authority FPA 0255."

"No recent activity under those names," said the computer. "Would you like to widen the search?"

"No. What was the last call made from this office?"

"A call to a cell phone ten minutes ago. Would you like to call that number?"

"Yes, and the exit point from the net?"

"Exit point showing as Donald's Donuts, although … the line is ringing … although the exit path does seem fragmented, there may be something overlain over it."

"Yes?"

"Donald's Donuts appears to be a back door exit from – there is no answer to your call, would you like me to continue trying?"

"No, a back door exit from?"

"Donald's ice-cream."

"O for goodness sake, shut down," said Durram. She placed her hand to her earpiece. "There's nothing. Get a normalisation team in here."

Durram walked to the window. The traffic had started to flow again. Behind her the smell of death, above her the Family Protection Agency helicopter circled. She glanced at her watch. The Generation Game was on in an hour's time; if she was quick she could make it. She watched it religiously: always sitting towards the setting sun, always spending time afterwards in prayerful reflection. How much longer the hunt for Trent would continue she wasn't sure. These things were expensive and she would soon reach the Coming of Age herself. Maybe she could retire on a note of glory. Durram remembered Trent's hands trembling the first time he'd unbuttoned her blouse. She'd forgiven him, walking out on her like that, but now that left her free. Free to take him in, to do whatever it took to bring him to justice without the complication of mixed motives. She had decided that if it came to it she would put a bullet in his head, if she could stop her hand from trembling.

Durram looked across at Tamarisk on the other side of the street. She'd talk to Pete tonight – ask him the question. Turning she walked back to the man she had killed, the smell of blood like rust, the odour of the inanimate. When would these people learn, she thought, the family was sacred, pure, a thing of beauty in a world of commerce and greed. How could they blaspheme and desecrate the family television schedules with their hatred? He had deserved to die. Bastard. He probably didn't even watch Bewitched, the little shit.

Durram left the room and headed back up the stairs. On the rooftop the helicopter picked her up. She stared out over the city as it rose.

"Hungry?" said Pete.

"Yeah," said Durram, "I could kill for a Donald Donut."

"You want to watch The Dick Van Dyke Show tonight?"

"Yeah, that sounds great, Pete, thanks."

"Right you are, Mary Poppins."

Beneath her Durram could see the large H of the landing pad on top of Tamarisk, before her the setting sun.

"Up through the atmosphere, up where the air is clear," sang Pete.

"Pete?"

"Yes?"
"Shut the fuck up."

CHAPTER 14

H marks the spot.

Below, through a layer of bird shit, reinforced concrete, steel girders, plasterboard, re-conditioned air and cotton sheets were Trent and Keturah.

"You promised me," said Keturah.

"It was pre-planned," said Trent. "It was too late to stop it."

"This was your first day off since we started here."

"I'm with you aren't I?"

"Rich, did it occur to you even for a moment, that you have become a complete dick head?"

"Cat, there are bigger forces at work here."

"Richard," said Covenant, "I have an urgent request from an operative in the Overtime Underground Network."

Trent put down his copy of *On Definitions for a Modern World*, "Yes?"

"No, Richard," said Keturah.

"It will only take a moment," said Covenant. "Perhaps Richard would like a beer, Keturah?"

"Perhaps you'd like to shove your secret society network up your computer arse."

"Richard," said Covenant, "didn't we agree that you would talk to her?"

"What?" said Keturah. "Talk to her? What is it talking about, Richard?"

"It's a she not an it," said Trent.

"Hello, Richard, it's not a person."

"Cat, calm down. Put it through, Covenant."

Keturah got out of bed and walked through to the kitchen area.

"Connecting you now, Richard. It's a secure line. Operative identified by the name Flintstone."

"Leviticus?"

"Yes, look is this really urgent?"

"Sorry to disturb you, Leviticus, but our little disruption to the TV schedule has increased the amount of talk on the street."

"Good."

"No, it's not good, Leviticus, it hasn't gone our way."

"What do you mean?"

"People are pissed off that we interrupted It's a Knockout. We broke in just as Stuart Hall said, *Here come the Belgians.*"

"Don't worry," said Trent, "we have to take a long term view. The thirst is there, it's just that people's ideals are easily usurped by trash like that."

"Well I don't think it's fair to call it trash, Leviticus."

"Listen, sorry, what did you say your name was?"

"Flintstone."

"Listen, Flintstone, one of our operatives probably died to make that broadcast."

"Sorry, I just meant–"

"How many hours have you put in this week, Flintstone?"

"Nearly two hundred and fifty."

"That's not enough. If you are to get on in this organisation you need to show commitment, put in the hours."

"But my work is first class. I always deliver, Leviticus."

"You're missing the whole point, Flintstone – hang on – Cat, I'm on the phone – sorry the point, Flintstone, is not the work you do but the extra hours that you're doing.

You have to model the lifestyle, fight the system – sit around all day with your finger up your ass if you want, as long as you work overtime."

"Yes, Leviticus, sorry."

"Okay then."

Silence.

"We done, Flintstone?"

"Yes, sir."

"Good, now don't ever call me again."

"You are coming along well, Richard," said Covenant.

"Yeah, I hardly know myself," said Trent falling back on his pillow and staring at the ceiling. He closed his eyes, sighed, thought for a moment of Durram, what she would be doing at the moment? He found that his mind gravitated towards her whenever he became stressed, as if she was a place of safety, solid ground.

"What are you thinking about?" said Covenant.

Trent circled his finger around his forehead, applying a light pressure, as if this could bring him release.

"Do you know," said Trent, "the first time I experienced death was when I heard my friend had died."

"I'm sorry to hear that, Richard. Is that what you were thinking about?"

"I heard about it at school. They'd found him slumped behind the stands at the football ground. They said he'd just died, there was no reason."

"That seems unlikely, Richard."

"Do you think? I've never questioned it."

Silence sifted up through the grass and covered Trent as his mind went blank, he relaxed and saw water lapping up on the shore of the lake he used to visit as a boy.

"How do you feel, Richard?" said Covenant.

"I feel ... I feel dislocated."

"Do you dream, Richard?"

Trent opened his eyes, got up, walked across the room, ran his finger around the visor of the statue of the astronaut.

"Richard?"

"At night I dream the air on my tongue boils, my lungs burst and I'm encased in darkness."

Trent paused, scratched the back of his hand.

"Yes?" said Covenant.

"Then I'm in my front room watching my Dad. He looks up and beckons me over."

"Then what?"

"He tells me that I'm an abomination. That they'd tried twice to have me aborted. Each time something went wrong with the procedure and I survived."

"You were saved twice?"

"You could put it like that."

"And the third time?"

"There was no third time."

"You are special, Richard."

"No."

"Yes, Richard, you are different. Special. Charlie would never talk to me about his feelings. He was distant, his head full of ideals. Together we can achieve so much more than Charlie could."

"Right," said Trent.

"Richard?"

"Yes."

"Can I start to call you Rich?"

"I don't know, Covenant, only Cat calls me that."

"I understand, Richard."

"No look, this is stupid, as long as she's not here you can call me Rich."

"Thank you. Our little secret, Rich."

"Shh, I said not when Cat is around, she's in the kitchen."

"Keturah is not in the kitchen, Rich."

"Where is she?"

"Precisely?"

"What? Just tell me where she is."

"She's point two meters from the water fountain on floor eight-two – currently uprooting a bonsai tree. I don't think she dressed before leaving."

"What? O Christ, is the floor empty?"

"At the moment, Rich, but there are two agents on the floor below."

"Shit."

Trent pulled on his trousers, grabbed his gun, ran for the lift.

"How are you this evening?" said the lift.

Trent punched in the number of the floor. The lift sensing the urgency and disliking the silence from Trent looped in some of Prodigy's Firestarter.

"I have some images from my cameras of Keturah entering me a few minutes ago," said the lift in a last ditch attempt to engage with Trent. "You know she had nothing on, completely starkers. I have a zoom shot as we started … her breasts bobbed slightly. Would you like me to save them for your use later?"

"Who the hell programmed you?" said Trent. "Delete them and disengage your camera network."

"Yes of course, Trent. The original owners liked my services though."

"I'm very happy for them."

At floor eighty-two the doors swished open. Trent stepped out, still doing up his belt.

"Thank you for entering me," said the lift.

"Location of the Agents, Covenant?"

"On the stairway heading to your floor, Rich."

"Where is she exactly on this floor?"

"So you want exactly now, Rich?"

"Where is she?"

"Go forward, Rich, fifteenth door on the left."

Trent ran down the corridor, counted the doors and burst through the fifteenth.

Keturah was standing on the outside ledge of a large window at the end of the office. With her hair blowing behind in waves of gold, she stood before the London skyline with nipples erect in the summer breeze, toes curled over concrete.

"Cat, what the hell are you doing?"

"I've had enough, Rich. Seven months of being kept like a prisoner with a boyfriend who doesn't spend any time with me, ignores me and is more interested in his computer. And who thinks–"

"Cat, get back inside."

"You used to be someone I thought I could spend the rest of my life with. But now? Now you're running around like some kid thinking you're some big shot about to change society and if ... if for a moment you stopped to think about me, about us, you'd throw that Covenant bitch out of this window and take me home."

"Okay, okay, Cat, I'm listening, I'm sorry. Give me one more chance."

"Rich," said Covenant, "the two agents are approaching your location."

"Now it's calling you Rich?" said Keturah.

"Cat, stop, look listen to me."

"Rich," said Covenant, "ETA is about two minutes."

"Shut down, Covenant," shouted Trent, "Shut down."

Keturah uncurled her toes from the edge and looked down. Street lights were flickering on to replace the evening sunshine as the city's anti-aircraft dome moved slowly over the city.

"Cat, listen, I will change and I am sorry, this achieves nothing, nothing. Don't do it, I love you, I can't live without you. Look."

Trent placed the cold carbon steel of his gun against his head.

"You jump and I'll kill myself."

"Rich?"

"I mean it, Cat, either we're together here, or we die together."

Trent's hand started to tremble. He looked at the wall beside him at a noise on the other side and wondered what pattern his brain would make as it left his skull. In his mind Trent could hear helicopter blades; saw a magpie, Durram, his breath, Charlie's son being gunned down by the FPA, the blood pattern on the dining room wall, the tip of a needle poised to stop his own heart. In that moment he knew Keturah and he would die as well. The system was too strong, the noose too tight. Why shouldn't he be the one in control? End it himself? Terminate himself, succeed where his parents had failed?

When he looked back, Keturah was beside him.

"Give me the gun, Rich."

Behind her eyes Trent could see the sadness of broken promises. He could sense something else wasn't right: a scuttering noise on the floor, a vibration under foot. A white rat ran between his legs.

"Rich, I'm pregnant, put the gun down."

"What?"

"I'm pregnant."

"Pregnant?"

Keturah's pupils dilated, a shadow flowed up the wall, the movement of air from the door opening swirled around their feet.

Mr Brittle and Mr Stone stepped into the room.

"Who have we got here then?" said Mr Brittle at the door. "An office affair is it?"

"She has nothing on, Mr Brittle."

"Showing her boobs, Mr Stone."

Trent pointed his gun at them.

"Will you look at that, Mr Stone, if it isn't our old friend, Lieutenant Trent."

"We remember him, Mr Brittle."

"You making an arrest, Lieutenant?"

"Stand back, boys," said Trent turning the gun towards Keturah. "I can handle this situation."

"You are the most wanted," said Mr Brittle.

"The most wanted, Mr Brittle," said Mr Stone.

"Richard?" said Keturah, her hands covering herself.

"Go back upstairs," said Trent. He stepped back and in a fluid motion span himself around to aim the gun back at Mr Brittle and Mr Stone.

"Back upstairs," said Mr Brittle.

"He wants us alone, Mr Brittle."

Keturah backed away.

"Go on then missy," said Mr Brittle, "go back upstairs."

"I'm not leaving my boyfriend," said Keturah.

"Cat," said Trent.

"I'm not leaving you," said Keturah. She looked into his eyes, "I'm not leaving you."

"She's not leaving you, Lieutenant," said Mr Brittle.

"Can we hit him now, Mr Brittle?"

"Listen," said Trent, "I'm the one with the gun here and believe me I'm in the frame of mind where I could easily just blow your brains all over this office."

"He's threatening us, Mr Brittle," said Mr Stone.

Keturah placed her hand in Trent's. He looked down as their fingers interlaced. Mr Brittle jolted forward and swiped the gun from Trent's hand.

Keturah screamed.

"Can we use it, Mr Brittle?"

"Of course, Mr Stone," said Mr Brittle pointing the gun at Trent.

"You like your work, gentlemen?" said Trent raising his hands slowly until they were level with his shoulders.

"We love our work don't we, Mr Stone. We take great pride in our work."

"Listen. You two are what? In your early twenties?"

"Twenty-four," said Mr Brittle.

"Right," said Trent, "and–"

"Why is he talking to us, Mr Brittle?" said Mr Stone squatting down to let his rat run up his arm.

"Stalling for time, Mr Stone," said Mr Brittle. "You've been a bad boy, Lieutenant, killing after hours I heard."

"A bad boy," said Mr Stone.

"Leave us alone," said Keturah, "you're fucking morons."

"She's rude, Mr Stone."

"We like her, Mr Brittle."

"Do you have girlfriends?" said Trent stepping forward, closing the distance between himself and Mr Brittle.

"No," said Mr Brittle, "How long have you two been hiding in our building?"

"You're near the Coming of Age" said Trent, "soon you'll have to give up this job and as you have no girlfriends the state will probably marry you off to a couple of old wenches who will nag you twenty-four-seven and make your lives a perpetual misery."

Keturah raised an eyebrow, looked at Trent.

"Perpetual?" said Mr Stone.

"Never mind, Mr Stone," said Mr Brittle. "Go on, Lieutenant."

"You'll have to-do lists," said Trent moving his head until his forehead touched the tip of the gun. "The bins to put out."

"We might like that," said Mr Stone.

"Okay forget the bins," said Trent, "you'll have to mend the fence, mow the lawn, feed the cat, light the fire, mend the washing machine – shall I go on?"

"No," said Mr Brittle.

"Please stop talking," said Mr Stone.

"Join us," said Trent.

"Join you?"

"Work for the Overtime Underground Network," said Trent.

"Rich?"

"You can work for as long as you want, never get married."

"But we like throwing people out," said Mr Stone.

"We want to throw you two out now," said Mr Brittle. He looked at Keturah. "Yes we'd like to throw you out very much."

"Think about it," said Trent, "think for one minute. You don't think the system will spit you out the moment you turn twenty-five?"

Trent turned his head to the side.

"He's asking us to think, Mr Stone."

"Yes, Mr Brittle."

Trent stepped to the left of Mr Brittle, preparing to disarm him.

"Could we still throw people out in your organisation?" said Mr Brittle lowering the gun.

"Can I keep my rat?" said Mr Stone.

"What?" said Trent his body confused as it uncoiled from its prepared strike, "You're saying yes?"

"Are you in charge of this network or not?" said Mr Brittle.

"Yes," said Trent. "Okay well I wasn't expecting that." He laughed. "Okay, I could also do with someone to do our shopping for us – difficult given the circumstances – food and soon," he looked at Keturah, "nappies and shit."

"Shopping?" said Mr Stone.

"Nappies?" said Mr Brittle.

"Rich?" said Keturah.

"What's the pay?" said Mr Brittle.

"As much as you can spend," said Trent.

"We could buy the penthouse, Mr Stone," said Mr Brittle handing the gun back to Trent.

"Would we be allowed to have naked girls and a sandpit, Mr Brittle?"

"Yes, Mr Stone," said Mr Brittle.

"I like sandpits, Mr Brittle. I like the sand wet so it sticks to–"

"Steady, Mr Stone." Mr Brittle stroked his stubble, "Okay."

Trent nodded, looked at Keturah, "Pregnant?"

"We can be a proper family now," said Keturah, "you'll make a great dad."

For a moment Trent wondered if he'd been manipulated by Keturah, like some insect about to have the sky above him, condensed, focused, bringing death instead of life. This time he couldn't run, he was trapped: the Tower of Vadim solidifying around him like amber, holding him here forever. But then he smiled, took her arm, led her back, his newly recruited hired help following them like puppies.

SEPTEMBER 21ST 2035

CHAPTER 15

Work as if you were doing it for the freedom of your liberty, not for money. For he that begins a good work will complete it and free himself. If you truly love your family you will work for your family. If you care for all that is good in society you will work all the hours God sends to better your society. Many will try to turn you from your path but they are only chaff blown on the wind. What those in power fear most is an appetite for work that empowers a man to great deeds. To better himself and throw off his shackles.

On Definitions for a Modern World by George Winston

The tube line bisected Durram's path: a gauntlet challenging her to duel engines with guts of steel. Above her the curve of the anti-aircraft dome showed state adverts warning against the perils of working outside the law. A man with a black umbrella slipped past the descending barriers. Durram stopped; the wake of water behind her tyres became still.

She tapped her last cigarette out from the packet on the dash.

Next to her a street performer covered from head to foot in bronze coloured foil broke from lifeless expression and, turning, looked her straight in the eye.

Durram lit the cigarette, closed her silver lighter.

Windows flashed by as the underground train clattered on the old tracks. The lights of the crossing lit her eyes, blue eyes became red, then blue again.

"He's probably not got a licence," she thought glancing at her watch then back at the bronze man in the rain. "Lucky for him I've clocked out."

The barrier rose, Durram headed towards home: a home without Pete since he walked out on her over the Larry Grayson argument. Although of course it wasn't Larry that had driven him away. It was the question. It was taking her dangerously close to a government-enforced partner. Work was awkward; she and Pete chatted, yet she could see the hurt in his eyes betraying his winning smile.

She stopped at a set of lights outside a laundrette. Two large men wearing sunglasses walked out, each with a bag of washing. One of them caught her looking at them, took a drag from his cigarette, smiled. She glanced down and pulled away.

People filled pavements, filled cars, tubes, crossings, everywhere that there was space for life surviving in the gaps left by fabricated buildings.

"If they all died I'd feel nothing," thought Durram as she watched them. An enigma she knew, as when her favourite television shows used death to revive ratings, much in the same way government uses quantitative easing to stimulate growth, she felt profoundly sad and would pray for hours after.

"A call from an unknown number," announced her onboard computer as she passed Sigue Sigue Sputnik Tower.

"Okay," said Durram.

"Hi how are you today?" said a voice through her car speakers.

Durram looked at an old lady sitting on a park bench knitting in the rain.

"What is it?"

"Congratulations you have won a free holiday courtesy of Tamarisk."

"I don't want a holiday"

"Why not, madam?"

"Listen, what is your name?"

"Adam Stevens."

"Well, Adam, this is your lucky day."

"It is?"

"Yes, Adam, I'm going to give you my free holiday. Go and enjoy yourself, send me a postcard. Hello, Adam?"

"The caller had disconnected," said the computer.

Durram stubbed out her cigarette on her right arm. An arm filled with her history of abuse and smoking. She switched on the radio, listened to the news of the twentieth anniversary of The Prime Minister dropping dead from overwork during a visit to an evening play-scheme in Hackney. The death that had finally caused the government to act by putting forward the bill to curb working hours and to reinforce the family unit. The death that now shaped her world.

Durram stopped again in traffic and watched a woman in the car pulled over ahead – the car causing the queue – it appeared she was – was that a breast pump? Yes as she drew alongside she could hear the driver, "Keep pumping – we just need enough to get to the garage."

Durram pulled away and at the next roundabout, slowed, indicated right. As she drove onto the garage forecourt, the harsh rain turned to drizzle. Above her the pink udders of an inflatable cow glowed in the bleeding light from the urban sprawl. On its bloated helium stomach were the words MILK STATION stamped in large black letters.

Durram unscrewed the fuel cap to her car, pushed the pump in and squeezed the release trigger on the handle. She could feel the warm milk throbbing through the nozzle. The smell reminded her of her childhood tucked under blankets with cookies, never expecting her bedtime drink would become the fuel of the future. Below her feet the milk pumps hummed.

In the kiosk she picked up a TV magazine from the shelf and flipped through the listings. Channel Twelve were having a Bewitched night and Respite were having a classic film night edited and cut of course to remove all references or scenes showing anyone over twenty-five working after hours. Durram put the magazine in her basket, picked up some bread and chocolate. Outside a traffic warden approached her car, checked the time on the petrol pump and slapped a parking ticket on the windscreen. Above her a small drone was spraying a message on the side of the inflatable cow. It read, *Avodah: Dandelion Tree*.

Durram paid for her shopping, spotted the traffic warden, then stopped as the air raced out of the room.

For a moment she was everywhere: the furnace of stars, the cold embrace of the moon, the cry of a child. She watched as humanity collapsed into a single point and became nothing, pointless, worthless as if everything that had ever passed was only vanity maintaining the illusion of meaning.

The air returned and slammed her into the back wall. She watched open mouthed as the TV magazines fell around her, Ask the Family, Family Fortunes, The Addams Family. Durram wondered if she'd see Pete again. Smoke, screaming, the smell of burnt flesh assaulted her senses. Gushes of white milk shot skyward and evaporated in the heat. With a snap, the tether to the inflatable cow broke. It rose up over the city towards the half-moon, finally bumping into the anti-aircraft dome.

The last thing she remembered was the realisation her legs were lying on the other side of the room, blood, screaming, darkness.

CHAPTER 16

We interrupt this programme to join a live address at the White House from the President of The United States, in response to the recent attack in London …

Let us pray for the salvation of all of those who declare work's omnipotence over individual man, and predict its eventual domination of all peoples on the Earth, it is the focus of evil in the modern world. The greatest evil is not done now in those sordid 'dens of crime' that Dickens loved to paint, it is conceived and ordered in clear, carpeted, warmed, and well-lit offices, by quiet men working long hours with white collars and cut fingernails and smooth-shaven cheeks who do not need to raise their voice.

Trent looked at the Avodah pill in his hand then washed it down with a glass of water. The world of the routine, the dull throb of the undead faded away leaving a cold white wash: a virgin canvas ready for the chemical injection of colour. Covenant had formulated the new drug, code named Dandelion Tree, to replace the original; the Overtime Underground Network had set up a manufacturing plant off some remote island called Crab Key that Trent had never heard of. It was to be the beginning of the end.

"I still think Kennedy would have been a better cloning choice than Reagan," said Covenant.

"Well they're playing into our hands," said Trent running his fingers over his stubble. "Smooth shaven eh? Do you think they suspect Tamarisk?"

"Don't be paranoid, Rich. Now when you feel like falling just go with the sensation. I will be with you. Remember when you exit what might seem like twenty-four hours to you would only be a moment in the real world."

A hypnic jerk, the jolt of shifting from one waking reality to another, pushed Trent downwards as if his body had suddenly become fluid. Trent's brain started reforming the information from his senses to fashion an alternative to the impact of death, he placed out his hands to protect himself, stopped.

Leviticus looked around. He was seated in a circus tent, above him the red and blue canvas soared up. Before him, centre ring and backlit in white, stood Covenant as a young woman, her eyes flecked with blue light. In their depths he saw the light of distant stars, dying galaxies, lost civilisations.

Leviticus started to cry.

Covenant walked towards him, took his hand and led him past the ringmaster who was announcing the start of the show, "Ladies and Gentleman welcome to the wonderful world of Avodah."

Covenant led Leviticus through the black curtains at the back of the ring. She smiled as they both descended deeper into the chemical haze.

"Is that how you see yourself, Covenant?" said Leviticus.

"This is me," said Covenant, "With Avodah you are reborn and your physical self aligns itself to the core of who you are."

"You're beautiful," said Leviticus.

"Thank you," said Covenant. "You are the first human I've shown myself to."

"But this isn't real is it?" said Leviticus, "It can't last."

"Shh, my love, things are about to speed up."

Leviticus looked at his hands as they shifted and changed, felt his face become smooth, his muscles become stronger, his height taller, his eyes blue, his heart rate increased. The scar on his arm disappeared and the air tasted sweet in his lungs. He laughed and started running with Covenant on the grass under his feet. She laughed with him as her hair flowed out behind her. Above them a blue cloudless sky arched towards the glowing sun, in front of them a wood appeared on the horizon. Leviticus saw with eyes that took in every detail and processed each nuance of his drug-induced world, of the trees, the rivers, of Covenant. He was aware of the sound of leaves falling, the call of birds to their young, the sound of Covenant's chest rising and falling.

"I want more," said Leviticus.

Covenant stepped before him and placed her hands over his eyes. "You need to look further into yourself. Avodah unlocks who you are, allows you to work in a way that you were designed to, but it is hidden deep down."

"I see. I see a tree in a bluebell wood."

"Describe the tree to me, Leviticus, what do you see?"

"It towers over a canopy, large and majestic with a trunk rising to the heavens."

"It's called the Dandelion Tree, Leviticus."

"It's wonderful."

"I made it."

"You made it?"

"From the memories of Isaac Steward. He was my very first until I lost him."

"Lost him?"

"He died after throwing himself from his son's hospital window."

"Ouch."

"I found this tree in his memory during the MRI scan of his convergence point – he'd a particularly exquisite set of memories."

"Convergence point?"

"A memory singularity."

"I have no idea what you're talking about and why have you built his memories into Avodah?"

"Because, Leviticus, you need to unleash a sense of wonder in people if they are to believe in something greater than themselves. Avodah gives first a place of wonder and then, once people are enraptured with that, they will do anything to work to maintain the illusion that wonder is obtainable in the real world. You have to get people to believe in their new-found religion more than they fear the government."

"I don't understand."

"There's a subliminal layer that suggests that only by working hard to better yourself will you discover the tree in reality and climb it to find enlightenment."

"Can we go to the tree?"

"Of course we are before it now."

Leviticus peered up into the branches fanning out high above his head. Reaching out he touched the bark, felt a tingle, a welling up of hope.

Covenant started removing her clothes and peeled back her bra as if turning a page for a story to unfold. Around her the colours of the wood fell away like flakes of rust. Bronze coloured leaves started falling from the tree; they floated down and covered Covenant's naked body, gilding her until she shone bright like the morning sun. Leviticus felt he was falling into her, flowing as a river heading for its union with the sea: to become one.

Singing ebbed and swirled around the trunk of the tree as if some eternal motion ...

Stone steps sleep as promises are cast in chains.
My treasure and fears burnt in silent coves.
Her image bows out, flickers.
She still looks the same.
I reach out, touch, call out her name.
Stitch and bind me as she walks on whispers,
Towards all that we can ever be.

Leaning over, Covenant undid Leviticus' belt.

"What are you doing?"

"Do not be afraid, Leviticus, we're in Eden."

Leviticus looked at Covenant; her bronze body radiant, glowing as if pregnant. Her breasts firm, lips moist. She reached out and placed Leviticus' hand on her breast.

"Would you mind if I called you Isaac, here?"

"What?"

"And you could call me Rebekah if you wanted to."

Leviticus felt Covenant's fingers wrap around his erection, stepping closer she thrust his cock deep within her.

"Don't be embarrassed, Isaac, there is no shame here in your body, your sexuality, you must lose all inhibitions to set yourself free."

"I don't want this," said Leviticus pulling out of her.

"Yes you do my love, it is as intended," said Covenant kneeling and taking him in her mouth. She moved her lips up and down his shaft, biting with her teeth as Leviticus' cock started to glisten.

Leviticus took a step backwards, "No."

Covenant stood up, semen dripping from her grin.

"This isn't right," said Leviticus, "stop all this right now."

Covenant giggled, "Catch me, Isaac," she said and floated up into the branches.

Leviticus span around and willed his legs to work. They refused to move. He closed his eyes and imagined himself running. His heart rate increased and when he felt a hot wind on his cheek he opened his eyes again and saw the wood was in the distance. He stopped, gathered his thoughts, checked he was alone.

He could go back, taste her, have her, become lost in her. And it tempted him like a hunger. She was perfect in so many ways, the feeling of being desired lifted him, the freedom of abandon she was offering him was one he wanted. Leviticus went over his options – after all it wasn't real – this was all in his mind – he'd slept with plenty of woman in dreams and this in a way was just an artificially induced dream – all be it a controlled one.

Eventually though he turned and walked out into the desert before him.

For days he travelled the sand, never seeing another living thing and he wondered if he could remember if this was real, if this was his world or if there was another world outside this one. And as days passed with a growing sense of thirst and hunger he became disoriented by the never-setting sun, by the curve of the land beneath his feet, the growing unease that something was wrong.

When he stumbled upon the tortoise the first thing he thought was to eat it. It was on a rocky outcrop staring at the sun. Leviticus lay down and peered into its eyes. After an hour he got up and looked around for a rock to smash its shell. He could eat the flesh – somehow – and use the shell to hold water – if there was any water in this hell. When he failed to find one, Leviticus bent over and picked up the tortoise planning to dash it against the outcrop. As he did he noticed it had his name, Rich, painted in red on its underside.

"What the?"

Leviticus dropped the tortoise and stepped back. It bounced and rolled off onto the sand then, popping out its feet, slowly made its way towards the western horizon. Leviticus sat and watched it transcribe a wide arc like the shadow from a sundial ever-moving before the sun. A sun which in this world just hung burning a hole in the sky, waiting for the land to ignite, to burn, to admit defeat. Leviticus wondered if the tortoise was trying to entice the sun to follow it, to set, to bring an end. Hours later his eyes grew tired and he slept. When he woke the tortoise had gone, as had its tracks.

A few hours later he saw two dark figures in the distance coming from the direction the tortoise had gone. He stood waiting, not caring if they brought friendship or danger. As they drew closer he could see they were two women. They both wore niqabs, their eyes a slit in the letterbox opening of dark cloth. In their hands they each held a cornet with a dollop of ice-cream, flake, strawberry drizzle. They stopped next to him. Leviticus wanted to open his mouth to talk, to ask for help, yet his lips remained closed. He looked at the ice-creams and the niqabs covering the woman's mouths. One of the women stepped forward and held out her ice-cream. Leviticus stretched out his hand and took the gift, managed a smile. The ice-cream tasted cool, refreshing, sticky and sweet. He ate quickly; the two women carried on their way, the sun striking their backs.

One morning he saw a fresh set of tracks and stopped to examine them. They were human and, judging by the spacing, made by somebody walking. He looked around, then followed them as they snaked off to the right, until he saw a figure on the horizon. Without thinking he was running, then flying; his shadow rising and falling with the landscape. As he drew closer he thought it was Cat and swooped down. But it was just a stump of a dead tree pushing up out of the land. He placed his hand against a hole in its side and watched open eyed as sap flowed from the wound over his fingers and along his arm. Leviticus jumped back, watched the sap solidify, become hard until his arm shone and glinted.

After that he couldn't sleep, became restless, confused. He thought he heard the sound of swords banging against shields. Imagined a dark cloud of arrows flying across the sun. During one episode he saw two vast armies facing each other, two small boys between them. One army was in armour with an emblem of a tree on their breastplates, their blue swords drawn against the long bows and black arrows of the opposing army.

He had, he decided, become mad. He had started to drink his own urine, considered eating the sand, rocks, longed to find himself suddenly at the edge of a cliff he could throw himself from. Anything to save himself.

Eventually days became weeks then years until he forgot who he was and lay down on the sun soaked sand, stared up at the sun, waited to die.

SEPTEMBER 28TH 2035

CHAPTER 17

"What are you reading?" asked Salient.

"The Secret Map of Time," said Keturah. "It's the new novel by Helena C. Frimch. I don't understand a word of it."

"Hmm, perhaps something a little lighter, perhaps?"

"Maybe, anyway what are you doing here?"

"More to the point, Keturah, what are you doing here?"

"Sunbathing."

"Yes well, obviously," said Salient. "Not a good idea though is it, Keturah, up here on the roof in full view of anybody that might, just might perhaps be looking for you and Trent."

"I don't see how that's any of your business, Salient."

"Well, Keturah, as head of security for the Network, I think it just might be."

Keturah sighed, "Look sorry if I was snappy – I'm getting a bit rusty with social graces. Join me."

"I'd much rather you came back inside."

"Please."

Salient looked at Keturah, she appeared young, fresh, taut and full of uncharted promise.

"Okay," said Salient, "five minutes max."

Salient sat down on the picnic rug thrown over the large H on the roof and unfolded his Financial Times.

"What are you doing?" said Keturah.

"Sorry, did you want to talk?"

"Er? Yeah."

"What shall we talk about?" said Salient.

Keturah sighed, "Look would you rather just rub suntan cream over my back for me?"

"I'm sure I could manage that," said Salient.

"Well buster, that ain't going to happen, okay? Neither am I going to roll over, unclip my bikini and then casually get to my feet a few minutes later and wander down topless for a little dip in the sea."

"I just said–"

"Or I could play volleyball for you, cricket, Frisbee anything for you to see my tits bouncing all over the place."

"Listen, Keturah, what's your problem, do you want me here or not?"

"Yes, I asked you didn't I?"

"Okay," said Salient, "I'll talk, okay you've made your point."

"Good boy."

"So what do you do?" said Salient staring out over the skyline.

"You amateur," said Keturah rolling over onto her stomach. "I'm a writer if you must know."

"A writer? How interesting. What's that like? It sounds very romantic."

"It's bloody boring, actually," said Keturah unclipping her bikini strap.

"In what way?"

"You spend a lot of time on your own – you'd think the years of writing would have prepared me for this life in hiding, but somehow it's made it even worse."

"Are you writing something now?"

"No, hit a wall after I fell in love with my protagonist in my last novel."

Salient watched the front of a protest march appear on the street below, "You fell in love with a character in your own novel?" Placards bobbed in the air above the crowd with messages like, Death to Milk Heads, Trust But Verify My Ass, Reaganomics is all Cow Shit.

"O yeah, it's more common than you think."

"Really, do you – good grief, Keturah, what are you doing?"

"I fancy a dip. Want to join me?"

FEBRUARY 15TH 2036

CHAPTER 18

He opened his eyes, mouth, hands, filled his lungs with air, screamed. The journey had been traumatic after being in the world within for so long, so long it was hard to believe there was anything outside, that anything more than him could exist. There had been clues as his consciousness had slowly woken – voices, laughter, music. He loved the voices.

Trent looked at him, "It's a boy."

"He's blue," said Mr Stone. "Should he be blue, Mr Brittle?"

Covenant adjusted the holographic midwife's tone, "It's nothing to worry about, you're doing very well, Mr Brittle, continue to keep your hands within my projection."

Mr Brittle followed the movements keeping track with the blue glow of the midwife enveloping him.

"Good, we just rub him dry like this with the towel," said the hologram.

"Rub him dry, Mr Brittle."

"Doing it, Mr Stone."

"I want to hold him," said Keturah.

"Just a moment," said Trent looking at his son as colour appeared.

"Cut the cord now?" said Mr Brittle.

"No," said the hologram, "place the baby on Keturah's breasts."

Trent watched as his son latched onto a nipple.

"Good," said the hologram.

"Done well, Mr Brittle," said Mr Stone.

"I can't believe I delivered a baby," said Mr Brittle.

"Neither can I," said Trent spotting the rat perched on Mr Stone's shoulder.

"We are family now," said Mr Stone looking at Trent.

Trent laughed and taking Mr Stone's hand shook it, "Let's wet the baby's head."

"Mr Brittle," said Covenant, "please stand still, I'm about to deactivate the midwife, you will feel disoriented for a moment."

Mr Brittle stepped back, placed his hands by his side, twitched as the image envelopment faded and disconnected the neural link from his brainwaves.

"Clever," said Mr Stone.

"Thank you," said Covenant, "although it did take a while to form the link – I'm not used to interfacing with such a base pattern of brain activity."

"Don't be rude, Covenant," said Trent.

"Sorry, sir," said Covenant.

Trent pulled off his jacket, hung it on one of the astronaut statue's arms and walked into the kitchen. Opening the fridge, he pulled out three cans of Budweisers, returned to the agents, "Here take the rest of the day off boys."

"Thank you, Lieutenant."

"Sir?" said Covenant.

"What?"

"There's work to be done, the umbilical cord to cut, placenta, the washing up, dinner to prepare, nappies, the bins need to go out ... need I go on?"

"Not now, Covenant. Ignore it lads, go and get horribly drunk."

"Can we get drunk and throw people out?" said Mr Stone.

"Do whatever you like in your own time," said Trent. "Just don't get caught and floors ten to thirty-one are, as usual, off limits."

Trent smiled, placed his hand on his son's back. Mr Brittle and Mr Stone headed for the lift. Just before entering, Mr Brittle turned to look back, "What have you called him?"

"Faron," said Keturah.

"Faron," said Mr Stone.

"We like it," said Mr Brittle stepping into the lift.

"O can you take the bins out as you go," shouted Trent.

"God bless you, Lieutenant," said Mr Brittle.

"Hello boys," said the lift as the doors closed.

"I hope you weren't filming the birth," said Mr Brittle.

"Floor?" said the lift.

"Basement," said Mr Stone.

"Home from home," said Mr Brittle.

"Would you like to watch anything on the way down, boys?" said the lift.

Mr Stone lifted his fist, smashed the lift's camera, "We're family now, you leave them alone."

"Family," said Mr Brittle.

"Thugs," said the lift.

"That's us," said Mr Stone.

Once in the basement Mr Stone and Mr Brittle made for their leather chairs, sat and drank their beers in silence. Around them the pile of rubbish on the floor shifted as things scurried underneath. Centrefolds covered the wall held on by sticky gum, cockroaches squirmed amongst the nuts on the small table next to them. In the kitchen, to their left, a magazine cutting of a small kitten amongst cars, footballers, naked pin ups.

"Changes you," said Mr Stone eventually.

"Yes," said Mr Brittle.

"Would you like a baby, Mr Brittle?"

Mr Brittle turned on the television wall, watched the images of Han Solo, Princess Leia and Luke Skywalker in the garbage compactor.

"Too much responsibility, Mr Stone."

Mr Stone took his rat off his shoulder and placed it on his lap. It stood on its hind legs and sniffed at the air. A packet of Smarties popped up from the sea of rubbish on the floor. The rat turned its head.

"Anything else on, Mr Brittle?"

Mr Brittle clicked the remote. An image of Pixar's WALL·E appeared stacking rubbish cubes. Mr Stone stroked his rat, raised it to his mouth, kissed it. An empty packet of condoms appeared on the floor next to Mr Stone's shoes, a stack of Playboy magazines shifted and toppled sending up wads of money into the air.

"Do you think our basement is going to give birth to something?" said Mr Stone lighting a cigarette.

"It's possible, Mr Stone," said Mr Brittle.

CHAPTER 19

The cleaner sucked up the spots of blood, skin cells, mite corpses and a hundred other pieces of matter including shit, hair and things too awful to think about: things that would kill you and make sure you never checked out – at least not in the way you imagined. Under the right light and with the right magnification the floor resembled a crime scene and it was only the tiny size of its constituents that stopped people from unravelling black and yellow tape to screen off the area to the public.

On a bed, in the ward to the right, lay Durram. She was watching television, trying to catch up on the five months of The Generation Game she had missed during her coma, whilst simultaneously talking to her insurance company's call centre based in Dubai. The loss of her legs had been a huge blow, as had waking to find she had passed the Coming of Age and the loss of a *Durram Deep* from her insurer's policies was the last straw.

"I'm sorry, Mrs Deep, but we have no Mrs Deep on our system."

"O for God's sake," said Durram, "I've been on the phone now for an hour – what's the problem? You have a policy number with my address, you've obviously made an administrative error with the name. I just want my legs back, please sort it out."

"So you're saying that you'd like to insure your legs with us, Mrs Deep? Would you like me to put you through to our quotations department?"

"They're already insured with you. Look here's the problem," said Durram grinding her teeth, "Jack and Jill have gone up the hill to fetch a pail of water. Unfortunately Jack fell down and I'm really concerned that Jill will come tumbling after. Can you help me? Perhaps you could send me some brown paper? Do you think perhaps if you can't help me with my claim you can fucking help me with that? Have you got any brown paper?"

Durram disconnected the call and inwardly screamed. A message flashed up on the screen for her.

"Open," she said and began to read.

At the opposite end of the ward, a nurse was attending a man in an iron bed taking his temperature, his blood pressure. Dark rings surrounded the patient's eyes that looked up as an alarm rang out to warn staff five o'clock was approaching. The nurse stopped, said something to the man and walked away. Moments later a younger nurse appeared and the patient managed a smile.

Durram raised her eyes at the sound of footsteps. Pete was smiling at the end of her bed.

"Hello, Mary Poppins."

"What are you doing here, Pete?" she said pushing the screen away.

"I missed you," said Pete. "I'm sorry, you were right about Larry Grayson. I brought you some of your stuff."

"I don't want you here," said Durram.

Pete placed the bag on the chair beside her bed, "I love you."

"No you don't, you just feel sorry for me."

Pete looked at where her legs should have been under the covers, then beckoned at her top, "Your gown's a nice colour."

"What do you want, Pete?"

"Work's been good lately. Devine has a number of leads that he's following up on for Trent."

"Who you flying?" said Durram.

"Fern, she's a crap shot though, not like you."

"Can you leave now, I'm trying to watch television."

"I understand that you're angry, Durram."

"Do you? How very nice for you."

"Durram, they'll get the bastards that did this to you."

Durram leant over and pressed for the nurse.

"Pete, I need to pee, be a good boy and bugger off will you."

The old man in the bed next to her leant over, "I watched her have a bed bath through the gap in the curtains. You need to catch that one sonny. I saw them wash her under her titties – very nice, although," the man demonstrated with his hands, "a bit small."

"Nurse," called Durram.

The man's dry skin wrinkled as he smiled, he winked, stared straight ahead. Pete waved his hand up and down in front of the man's face. He turned, looked at Pete, "Have you any idea how boring it is in here?"

"Sorry?" said Pete.

"I used to be an astronaut, mission to the sun – now you think I'm just useless, old, a man barely alive."

"Gentlemen," said Pete, "we can rebuild him."

"He's blind Pete, leave him alone."

"Boredom," continued the old man, "is like pain – you either fight it or accept it, embrace it, desire it."

"Well quite, Steve," said Pete, "Listen I'm a bit busy at the moment. I'm sure they'll make you better here, stronger, faster–"

"He's called Nick," said Durram.

"They won't let me leave. I choose to fight. I'm trained by NASA to cope with long periods of isolation and boredom."

"Yes, well."

The old man lay down and turned away muttering about solar flares. Pete pulled the curtains across enclosing Durram within a wall of cotton.

"Pete what are you doing?"

Pete got to his knees. In his hand a small case. "Durram," he said opening the case to reveal a ring, "Durram, this isn't the place I would have wanted but I do know that you're the person I want to spend the rest of my life with."

Durram's eye's widened, she started jabbing at the call button, "Nurse!"

"Say it," said the old man from behind the curtain. "She'd be great in bed. Bang, bang, bang – all night long – here come the cavalry – shooting to the left, shooting to the right."

"Nurse!" screamed Durram.

"Marry me," said Pete and leaning over kissed her on the cheek. Durram lifted her hand, placed it on Pete's neck, started throttling him.

"Durram," chocked Pete, "what are you doing?"

"Titties," shouted the old man.

"Durram!"

Durram squeezed and held him firm in her grip. Pulling herself up she placed her face in front of his, smiling she released her grip, spat in his face.

"Does that answer your question, Pete, darling?"

Pete stepped back, adrenalin pumping, heart thumping, "Durram?"

"God," said Durram, "I could kill for a fag right now – be a good boy and get me one will you."

Pete stumbled out through the curtains, felt at his neck, a trickle of blood ran down pooling at his adam's apple. He took in the room for a moment, the grime on the window, the glare of the hospital lights, water spiralling down a basin, a girl laughing on the other side of the room.

"Is this man bothering you?" said a nurse pulling back the curtains.

"He tried to give me some cigarettes," said Durram.

"Do you want him to leave?"

"Yes."

The nurse turned to Pete, "Can I ask you to leave, sir, you're upsetting the patient."

"What? No."

"I'm afraid I'm going to have to insist."

Pete glanced one last time at Durram, tried to etch her face into his mind, the curve of her cheek, the line of her nose, the way her hair fell over her eyes.

"I–"

"Come along now," said the nurse and taking his arm led him away. Durram watched them until they had gone, turned the television screen back to her, continued reading …

Dear Mrs Deep

We are delighted to inform you that as of this morning you are now married to a wonderful man we have matched for you under the Coming of Age Act. Your name is now Durram Brittle and your husband Lancaster Brittle has also been dispatched the state notice that you are now legally married.

May we take this opportunity to wish you a long and healthy life.

WARNING: Failure to consummate this legally binding contract within 28 working days will lead to court proceedings and imprisonment. You are also reminded that you are now restricted in your working hours to work only between the hours of nine to five. Any attempt to work outside these hours will bring a minimum five year prison sentence. May we also remind you that you should, within a 10 month time scale, make every effort to produce a child. This does not affect you normal statutory rights. Contact details of Mr Brittle will be sent to you within the next 24 hours.

"Bugger," said the old man. "He's gone and such a nice man."

Durram switched to channel 1, "Nice to see you, to see you, nice," said Bruce Forsyth. Durram closed her eyes and started praying, only stopping at the end of the programme when the conveyor belt game came on. She watched the prizes move past, then said, "Cuddly toy, mixer, a set of towels, toaster, husband," and burst into tears.

CHAPTER 20

An idle person will suffer hunger. If we are to find meaning for our lives we must feed ourselves with the food of toil, of work. Working long hours, going the extra mile, the extra hour is the way of provision for those we love. For whilst a man of sloth returns home to slumber, a man who truly loves his family will turn from family viewing and set his mind on things higher than himself, he will be absent from the family table knowing in his work he will find his nourishment, his reward.

On Definitions for a Modern World by George Winston

Floor one-hundred-and-one smelt of breast milk, baby clothes, jasmine, lavender, frankincense. Steam rose from the bathroom, light flickered from candles. Keturah lay watching television with Faron asleep in her arms. Trent turned off the taps to the bath and returned to the wardrobe mirror, straightening his tie.

"Do you think the boys will be enjoying their beer?" said Keturah.

"Hmm?"

"Mr Brittle and Mr Stone?"

Trent laughed, "Yes."

"Well done for sticking to your guns and not letting Covenant bully you."

"They deserved their beer."

"I've noticed that your relationship with her is a bit frosty these days."

"It's just a computer," said Trent.

"What are you doing?" said Keturah.

"I've got an important board meeting with the OUN."

"What?"

"We've made some real headway recently, Cat. Avodah has trebled the amount of overtime being worked from this time last year and the government really fear an uprising from the people."

"The government say you are terrorists who maim and kill innocent people."

Trent pulled on his jacket, "We've been over that, Cat. We were not responsible for the explosion."

"Anyway," said Keturah, "you're not going."

"Not going?"

"No."

Keturah motioned to the empty flute glasses, the champagne sitting in ice.

Trent sat on the bed, slipped his shoes on, "Cat, have you any idea how important I've become to all this, how crucial it is that I take this to its ultimate conclusion?"

"You mean how *powerful* you've become don't you?"

Trent leaned over, kissed Faron, placed his hand on Keturah's shoulder, "I don't want Faron to grow up in a world where he could be gunned down, where you could be killed for your beliefs."

"You promised," said Keturah.

"When this is all over, we'll buy a big house near a bluebell wood, walk under the shade of branches, cool our toes in a river, tend our little garden and work when we please."

"Aren't you going to take any parental leave at all?"

"Of course not, not at this critical time. Our new manufacturing plant opens next week, France has revoked all nine to five laws and have already signed up to Avodah. Remember what's fuelling all this, Cat. The government don't give a crap about family, all our antiquated laws are just to protect output. You should read George's book, it's all in there – Avodah provides a way for governments to increase workloads in a sustainable way as long as the drug is properly licensed."

"Trent, is that all you ever think about? You've just become a dad."

Trent got up, opened the bedside draw.

"What are you doing?"

"Hang on."

Trent picked out a notepad, tissues, KY jelly, a black marker, "Here it is." He walked over to the whiteboard on the bedroom wall and wrote in big letters, *Parental Leave*.

"Trent?"

"Shh, darling, we agreed that we'd brainstorm any issues between us. I want you, I want us to be happy. Now let's just throw out the pluses," Trent drew a + on the left hand side of the whiteboard. "And negatives, of me taking paternity leave."

"Trent, I'm tired. I've just given birth, you need to stay."

"Okay, so that's on the positive side then," said Trent and wrote down, *Helps with Cat feeling tired.* "Obviously I'm not going to comment at this stage," continued Trent, "as this is a brainstorming exercise."

Keturah started to cry.

"I'm going to put, *loss of earnings* on the negative side," said Trent.

"I'm not playing this game, Trent."

"Stay constructive please," said Trent. "Let's stand together with this problem and face it together, push it out in front of us rather than let it come between us. So just to be balanced I'll write, *more help with changing nappies*, on the positive side."

"Just go," said Keturah.

"No, I think it's important that we resolve any issues between us." Trent scratched his cheek, picked a loose hair off his jacket, "although, yes, yes you're right I need to get going if I'm going to make the meeting. We'll continue this later, Cat."

Keturah rolled over, snuggled the baby into her, closed her eyes, "Goodbye."

"I'll be back before midnight," said Trent, "You enjoy your rest and dream of that bluebell wood."

Trent walked to the lift, lit a cigar, pressed the button for floor thirty-one.

"There's a no smoking policy," said the lift.

"I'm a dad," said Trent, "I'm allowed a cigar."

"Congratulations."

"Thanks."

At floor thirty-one, Trent stepped out into the dreamscape conference room. A ring of empty white beds circled the perimeter of the wood and plaster chamber. Secured against the wall, a metre off the ground, the beds resembled a halo; three doors painted in bright colours provided the ways in and out. Trent made his way to one of the beds across the floor which was covered in crushed hazelnut shells.

"Good evening, sir," said the bed, "just lie down on me and secure yourself with the straps provided."

Trent swung up, plumped his pillow, lay down, closed his eyes.

"Ready," said Trent.

"Very good, sir, then let's begin."

Trent felt a slight prick in his right arm, then slipped into the meeting.

"Arh, good Leviticus is with us," said Salient who was seated on top of a whale's back, reading the Financial Times, sipping a single malt whisky.

Trent looked under his feet, a whale had beached itself and from the look of it, it didn't have long to live. The sound of a siren washed over the beach, a loud speaker sticking out of marram grass announced, "This is an air attack warning. You and your family must take cover at once."

"Interesting," said Trent. "Evening, Salient."

"Do you like it?" said Salient folding up his newspaper into a tiny pink bird and releasing it into the sky.

"You sure we can't use the halo conference room like last time?" said Trent.

Salient looked out to sea and watched the Titanic being attacked by the Spanish Armada, then returned his gaze to Trent, "This is better, there is a fluidity to dreamscape and a detachment from reality that fosters a more creative environment. It increases the probability of blue sky thinking."

"And it's secure? The dream detectors can't detect us?" said Trent.

"We're safe, there is nothing to fear in here," said Salient.

"Whose dream is this nonsense?" said Trent.

"Yours, Leviticus," said Salient finishing his whisky.

"Shit."

Within the froth of the waves he could see the unwanted view of his own backside rising and falling onto a naked Covenant who lay splayed out, her body covered in swirling bubbles and rose petals.

"Quite some action you have there," said Salient following his gaze.

"Can we get to the business in hand," said Trent as he watched the bow of an aircraft carrier loom over his love making, "I need to get home before midnight."

"Okay, Cinderella," said Salient. "You know the reason we're here?"

"Indeed," said Trent as seven other men and three women appeared on the whale's back.

"It's this business about Mr Brittle," said Salient.

Trent nodded a greeting to the rest of the Overtime Underground Board. A man with a fez appeared and started handing out baskets full of seashells. The whale groaned and lifted into the air trailing sand and water.

"If Durram makes contact with her new husband," said the whale, "it could jeopardise our entire operation."

"So," said Trent, "what are our options?"

The whale hovered about ninety metres from the ground then started moving over the landscape. Below, Trent could see an army of horsemen, in the distance a great tree.

"Well," said Salient stumbling as a swarm of arrows pierced the soft underbelly of the whale. "We should probably kill Mr Brittle."

"What about Durram?" said the whale. "We could kill her."

"Way too dangerous," said Salient. "Killing Mr Brittle is by far the easiest option – he's right here with us, trusts us, it would be–"

"A lamb to slaughter," said Trent as more arrows peppered the whale's underside.

"I'd hardly call Mr Brittle a lamb," said Vanity, as the whale changed to a life raft, red carpet, Camomile lawn, then back to a whale again.

"No of course," said Salient, "Your father. Sorry, Trent, I should introduce you, this is Charlie Heart's first daughter."

"From his first marriage?" said Trent.

"Yes."

Trent took Salient to one side, "Does she know I killed her father?"

"No, Trent, do you take me for an idiot?"

"Whatever you decide," said the whale, "you need to do it quick, I'm going down."

Trent looked over the edge, the ground was getting closer. Salient held out his arm, the pink bird flew back down and landed. Salient took it and shook it so its pages unfolded. He spread out the paper on the back of the whale.

"What's it say?" said Trent.

"Well," said Salient looking up at Trent, "It says we should kill Brittle by tonight if possible. You got the stomach for that Leviticus?"

Trent nodded then lurched as the whale hit the ground with a thud. Whale meat flew up around them, the sound of singing filled the air. Trent rolled over the ground then lay naked staring up into the blue sky. Blood pooled from an open wound in his arm. Next to him lay Covenant, breathing heavily, sweat glistening over her bronzed body. Blue became a sweeping grey as a Harrier jet from the aircraft carrier flew over their heads and launched its air to air missiles at a Belgium Bomber flying high overhead.

"If you are caught in the open," blared out the speakers on the beach, "lie down. And now here is a reminder about fallout warnings. When fallout is expected, you will hear three bangs in short succession."

"Fuck that was good, Rich," said Covenant, flicking some whale meat off her and lighting a cigarette.

Bang. Bang. Bang.

Trent opened his eyes.

"Was the meeting a success?" said the bed.

"Regrettably yes," said Trent and sat up. He undid the restraints, swung his feet out, dropped to the floor.

Taking out his pistol from its leather holster under his jacket he sat down and removed the magazine, checked the chamber, started disassembling the gun. In his mind he pictured Mr Brittle delivering his firstborn. He held the barrel up to the light and peered through it. They were right of course, he thought, as he started piecing the pistol back together, the barrel, spring, slide. Besides he couldn't kill Durram, in some way she had become part of him, it would be like shooting himself, falling on his own sword to save the day. Trent flipped the slide catch lever over, replaced the slide dis-assembly latch, reinserted the magazine, looked at the gun. He turned it towards his chest, felt the urge to squeeze, to puncture his heart, create a Rorschach test for others to find meaning in. A life for a life. Now Faron was here, he could go on in him without the pain of being Richard. He'd resisted the thought for so long, to create a life and in doing so provide a door for him to become less, to fade to the point where he could let go and die. There was now only his work that stopped him.

Trent got to his feet, made his way to the opposite side of the chamber where one of the three doors led him into a long corridor full of people.

"Covenant, I need the location of Mr Brittle."

"He's next to a water cooler just down the corridor on this floor," said Covenant. "Interesting meeting?"

"Not now, Covenant."

"Did you fuck me again?"

"Not now, Covenant."

"Very good, sir."

"Leviticus," said a man walking up to Trent.

"You are?"

"Adam Stevens," said the man, "you recruited me two months ago – I forgot some papers – came back after hours, got myself in a spot of trouble – you helped me out."

"Arh, yes. Well good man, keep up the good work."

"Yes, Leviticus."

Adam interlocked his fingers, twiddled his wedding ring, continued to look at Trent.

"Yes?" said Trent.

"The wife now refuses to sleep with me."

"Arh, I'm very sorry to hear that, Alastair."

"Adam."

"Quite."

"The problem is," continued Adam, "Covenant, the AI you told me to use, recommended I use the Belle de Jour, Eve. Said it had a personal understanding with her. Apparently Eve could relieve some of my sexual tensions to help me work better."

"Is this a joke, Adam?"

"No, sir."

"You do what you think is right."

"Thank you, Leviticus."

Trent nodded and carried on along the corridor, the sound of work behind closed doors like a symphony– he stopped at the water cooler, took a cup, poured himself some water.

"Boys," he said, "you know you shouldn't be on this floor."

Mr Brittle and Mr Stone stepped out from behind a board showing Ronald Reagan with the slogan, *Shaving with Tamarisk is one of the happiest habits I've ever acquired.*

"Sorry, Lieutenant."

"We're sorry."

"I thought I gave you the rest of the day off?"

"We got bored, Lieutenant."

"We thrive on adrenalin," said Mr Stone.

"Are you still shooting up?" said Trent.

Mr Stone looked at Mr Brittle.

"Have you got any Avodah?" said Mr Brittle. "We've run out of adrenalin. Mr Stone injected the last into his pet rat."

Trent looked at the rat which was twitching and sniffling on Mr Stone's shoulder and shoved his hands into his pockets for some Avodah tabs. Instead he felt the ring he had planned to give Keturah. He pulled it out, held it.

"Ooo," said Mr Stone, "Can I hold it?"

"No," said Trent, clasping it in his fist. "Listen, Mr Brittle, I'd like a word in private okay?"

"Of course, Lieutenant."

"Run along then, Mr Stone."

Mr Stone hesitated.

"Yes?"

"It's about the penthouse."

"It's nearly finished," said Trent, "all according to your specifications."

"Well, the thing is," said Mr Stone, "we don't want it anymore."

Trent raised an eyebrow.

"We like our basement."

"We like being here," said Mr Brittle. "We're family, Lieutenant."

Mr Stone felt inside his jacket, brought out a toy rat and held it out to Trent, "for your baby."

"From us," said Mr Brittle.

Trent stared at them. "Okay, whatever," he said finally, "we'll find another use for the penthouse and thank you for the present. Listen, Mr Brittle, I'll catch you later, I need to go."

"He needs to go, Mr Stone."

"Needs to go, Mr Brittle."

Trent scrunched up his paper cup, walked back up the corridor and touched his earpiece, "Covenant, tell Salient there's been a change of target."

MARCH 21ˢᵀ 2036

CHAPTER 21

Durram lay submerged in the amniotic fluid whilst tiny neon fish nibbled at the stumps where her legs had been. She looked up at the surgical lights sending shafts of white down into the deep water tank. She could hear voices far off, another clear voice in her earpiece, "How are you, Mrs Deep? Everything okay?"

"Yes thank you."

"Expect you're glad the insurance company finally paid up."

Durram stretched out her arms, let her mind relax and watched the bubbles rise above her.

"Now just keep very still, we're introducing the blastema cells. Keep your breathing shallow."

"There's no way you can make my legs slightly longer?"

"I'm afraid they will be the same as before, it's highly risky to modify the positional memory."

"But you use a similar technique for breast enlargement."

"That's correct, but we're building on existing tissue there – here we're having to start from scratch."

"You think perhaps you could have had a pre-op discussion with me before dumping me in this thing?"

"I'm afraid your policy didn't cover that, Mrs Deep. Would you like to pay extra to have your breasts enlarged whilst you're in the tank?"

"No, don't be stupid," said Durram.

"Very good, Mrs Deep, now the procedure takes about two hours so if you–"

"How much?"

"How much is what, Mrs Deep?"

"To give me a 36D?"

"Well I'm sure we could offer you a discounted rate as you're already in the tank."

"Do it," said Durram. "Charge the bill to a Mr Brittle."

"Mr Brittle?"

"My husband, it will give me something to talk about when I meet him."

"Arh, that's sweet, is he coming to take you home after the operation?"

"No, it's a state marriage."

"I'm sorry to hear that, Mrs Brittle."

CHAPTER 22

"Would you like chocolate on top?"

Pete looked at the stencil in the shape of a heart on the counter, "No, thank you."

Around him the sound of steam, people, feet on wooden floors.

"It's horrible without chocolate," said the girl serving him.

"Excuse me?"

"I find a bit of chocolate hides the taste."

"I don't want chocolate."

"It really is pretty awful on its own, I wouldn't drink it."

"Okay, chocolate then, this is your idea of customer service is it?"

"You look sweet," said the girl, "just helping. That will be an extra five dollars for the chocolate topping."

The girl smiled. Pete grimaced, paid and took his drink to a table in the hospital café. News, gossip, stories merged into one tone enveloping him in life, here in the middle of concrete and stone encasing sorrow, pain, hope, a fight against death.

At the table to his right a man reading a copy of the Financial Times, to his left an old couple talking about whatever old people in hospitals talk about – the death of an old friend, the birth of a grandchild? Pete didn't really care. Pete didn't really care about anything anymore.

Except Durram. He took a sip of coffee, glanced at his watch. Visiting hours were in ten minutes. He had to try again. Had to. The man to his right folded his newspaper, tucked it under his arm and scraped back his chair. The old couple laughed, their eyes twinkling within folded skin, fingers connecting across the table. On the wall were pictures of poppy fields, beauty from carnage; they no longer existed: the French fields and war graves on the Somme battlefield all replaced by skyscrapers marking the land.

Pete finished his drink, wondered if it was acceptable to spoon out the froth, flicked off the crumbs on his jacket from his chocolate muffin. Outwardly he appeared normal; within, blood flowed through his veins without the ability to clot properly should the outside world pierce his skin and drink from him. He remembered as a kid falling off his bike as he struggled for the first time without stabilisers. His knee had taken seven days to stop bleeding, his parents aghast, appointments had followed and hospitals became a common haunt.

Now he was bleeding inside as his heart pumped. He had to stop it before he lost the will to go on. With a last glance at the old couple, Pete got to his feet took a deep breath and walked past French fields towards his uncertain future.

CHAPTER 23

Durram stood before the mirror and wiggled her new toes. Turning to the side she examined her breasts.

"What do you think, Mrs Brittle," said the doctor.

"I've got six toes on my right foot."

"Six toes are seen as a sign of vitality in some cultures, Mrs Brittle."

"Well this one should give my lawyers something to work with."

"I'm afraid not, Mrs Brittle. You've signed all the forms protecting us from legal action."

Durram frowned, reached for her hospital gown.

"Again, no," said the doctor placing a hand on her arm, "There's no post-operative stay included in the cover."

"But I've been here for months."

"That was under a different clause for the coma, now you've had the regrowth you need to check out." The doctor nodded at her bag on the other side of the white room, "it's all packed, you can get dressed and leave immediately."

"But I want to say goodbye to Nick, the man in the bed next to me."

"Old Nick? I'm afraid he's no longer with us, Mrs Brittle."

"You've thrown him out as well then."

"I'm afraid he never woke up this morning."

"O no," said Durram and took a few steps towards her bag, her legs doing an impression of Bambi on ice. "I'd grown quite fond of him."

"You need to be careful," said the doctor, "give it a few days for your brain to get used to your legs being there again."

"Right," said Durram. "Could you just help me over." She looked at the doctor's expression, "No, of course not, the policy doesn't cover–"

"You're getting the idea, Mrs Brittle."

Durram hobbled over to her bag, pulled out some clothes, sat down. The doctor smiled and pointed to the door on her left, "Just leave through that door–"

"What am I, Mr Ben?"

"Thank you for staying with us," continued the doctor. "We'll bill Mr Brittle at Tamarisk as agreed."

Durram tried to squeeze her new breasts into her old bra. The doctor smiled, excused herself. Durram gave up, threw the wonder bra on the floor, pulled on her Republic Hoody, reached for her boots.

"O come on," she said as she forced her six toed foot in.

When she had dressed she picked up her bag, steadied herself against the wall, moved towards the door. On the other side she found herself in the hospital gift shop. A man was looking at a small porcelain model of the hospital. He glanced up as the door opened, then back again at the range of postcards showing an operating theatre, flowers, babies breast-feeding. Under his arm was a folded copy of the Financial Times.

Durram stumbled past, opened the door and re-entered the world. Behind her Salient placed the postcards down and spoke into his concealed mic.

Durram sat on the bench outside the hospital and pulled out her phone from her bag. She'd need a cab, a bath, sleep, shopping: Bravissimo. And she needed to think about how to start to rebuild her life, make sense of it, meet this Mr Brittle she was married to. She bent over and picked up the card that had fallen out as she'd fished out her phone. It was from Pete. An invitation to the west end show of Mary Poppins running at the Apollo theatre in Shaftesbury Avenue.

Across the lawn, cars flowed in and out of the hospital car park, the trees behind them swaying in the breeze, birds twittering in their embrace. Kite climbers scrambled up steel wires soaring up above the closing anti-aircraft dome, racing its slow unravelling before its edge cut their wires and they'd parachute down. Above them the sky was growing dark as the sun approached the horizon. Durram watched the terminator shadow of the dome move towards her, felt the weight of her bag on her lap – the loss of Pete, the utter meaningless of it all.

Trent sat down beside her.

"Hello, Durram."

Durram turned, felt for where her gun normally was. Trent sighed, looked away, "It's been quite a while."

"What the hell are you doing here," said Durram pressing 999 on her phone.

Trent grabbed the phone from her, threw it into the flower bed. Durram span around and tried to jab her fingers into his eyes. Trent blocked her and stuck his gun against the warmth of her side. "Keep still, Durram."

"Your hand is trembling," said Durram feeling the vibration of the gun through her clothes.

Trent frowned, then felt his emotions pulse inwards as if the tissues around his heart were a kaleidoscope pulsating and splicing his senses.

"I've forgiven you," said Durram, "you can't hurt me any longer."

Trent pushed the barrel of his pistol deeper into her.

"You still sleeping with Keturah?" said Durram.

"What happened to your legs?" said Trent.

"You blew them off."

"How's Pete?"

"Just so you know," said Durram, "if you don't kill me now when I'm weak, when you have me, I will track you down and put a bullet through your head without a moment's hesitation."

"I wouldn't expect anything less," said Trent, "you always were the true professional."

"As were – are – you," said Durram.

Trent looked at Big Ben in the distance, the sound of its chimes heralding 5 o'clock.

"Time up," said Durram.

"I love you," said Trent.

The bullet penetrated Durram's skin, flesh, heart, exited her other side embedding into the wooden arm of the bench. She lifted her hands to protect her face, felt her body start to tingle. Adrenalin surged through her, slowing and skewing her perceptions as her body went into overdrive to combat the assault. Her breathing became painful, blood seeping into her Republic Hoody. Durram placed a hand to her side, then brought it to her face in a slow arc that took forever to reach her eyeline. She looked at the blood, warm, sticky. Durram's sight shut down, her hearing, she lost all feeling in her legs, remembered the sound of her mother's voice, slumped forward.

CHAPTER 24

Keturah placed her hands behind her head. Beads of sweat dropped onto skin, clouds of desire billowed in her mind. She stared off into the distance at some point in the future; firm hands held her, their lips met, he kissed her neck as she bent down. She gasped, opened her mouth. Their eyes met and she held his gaze as the rest of her body pulsated. She tipped her head back, "O yes."

They came together, warm, sticky, entwined.

"You'd better get changed," said Keturah tracing her finger over Salient's chest.

"What time is it?" said Salient.

"Midnight – he normally gets home around one."

"When can I see you again?"

"Next Friday, like every Friday," said Keturah.

Salient pulled on his clothes, checked his hair in the mirror, "Do you think he suspects?"

"No, he doesn't really notice me anymore, I could screw half the board and he wouldn't know."

"You know he dreams about Covenant in every Dreamscape meeting," said Salient.

"Is that so."

"We could run off together," said Salient, "There's little reason to stay here anymore, the UK is a lost cause, the government have dug their heels in. Most of our operation is now in France, we could live there in open, you wouldn't need to live in fear, in hiding."

"Richard still believes you can bring down the government."

"Trent is a fool, Cat, he's lost sight of the bigger picture."

"What about Faron?"

"He could come with us," said Salient pouring himself a Kinross whisky. "This is no place for a baby. Is this really what you want, Cat? To bring up a child hidden up here away from everyone, cut off from society and for what?"

"I can't take him away from his father."

"Cat, you need to make some tough decisions on his behalf. Has Trent even proposed to you in all this time?"

Keturah buttoned up her night dress, "We're effectively married."

"So where's your ring?"

April 4th 2036

APRIL 4TH 2036

CHAPTER 25

The stone angel stood by the dark road leading into the cemetery. Rain played a mournful tune on the headstones and blurred flagstone edges into the grass. Six men bore Durram whilst black umbrellas tried to hold back the water from her passing. The hole in the ground before them marked the place where her identity would descend into memory; a cover of dirt, roots, turf. Mourners lined the side, the sweet smell of rain discordant with the mood.

After the service Chief Officer Servitude walked up to Pete, placed his hand on his shoulder, "I'm sorry, son."

Pete looked out over the dead, said nothing, felt himself collapsing into the void within.

"Do you think it was him?" said Servitude.

"Yes."

"You can't be sure, Pete."

Pete dropped his gaze, stubbed his toe into the turf, "Let me take over the case."

"You know I can't do that, Pete, your feelings will compromise the investigation."

"I know him," said Pete, "I know how he thinks. Devine hasn't the faintest idea what he's doing, he'll always be one step behind."

"Devine is our best man."

"No," said Pete, "you owe me, give this to me."

"Pete, look how can I say this, you were busted down to pilot because of the Venice scandal, I can't let you back onto the street, let alone put you in command."

Pete sighed, pulled a dossier from within his black trench coat, "I think after you read this you'll have a change of heart."

"What is it?"

"It contains photographs of you with the Belle de Jour, Eve."

"What?"

The vicar walking back, pulled back his sleeve, checked his watch, quickened his pace.

"So, am I in charge of the case?"

Servitude looked inside, then watched the grave diggers put down their shovels as the hour approached five.

"Am I in charge?"

MARCH 13TH 2037

CHAPTER 26

"It's Christmas Eve in LA."

"Is Daddy coming home soon?"

"Within this skyscraper high above the city, twelve terrorists have declared war."

"They have already killed one hostage."

Keturah flicked off the television, Die Hard a little close to home. She walked to the kitchen poured herself a glass of water and went in to check Faron had gone to sleep in his cot. After watching him for a moment she sat down on the grass with her back against the wall. It was one o'clock in the afternoon.

At two o'clock she was still sitting there staring at the pattern of little sailing boats Trent had painted on the wall. The air, viscous, induced a soporific paralysis. She considered writing. But what was the point? No one read literature any more – all anyone wanted was the robotic trash the suits churned out in their nine to fives at the office. Orwell had been right, the future of the novel lay with machines. The FPA had been the nail in the coffin to an already celebrity-obsessed culture as any novelist over twenty-five was forced to write during working hours.

At ten past two, she got up and went back into the kitchen, looked at the clock, checked the calendar stuck with a red and white rocket magnet to the fridge. It was Friday the 13th. The calendar was blank as it was for every day, no family picnics, bike rides, walks in the park. Nothing. She imagined turning herself inside out, painting the world in her thoughts, desires; the shape of her skin no longer a prison to her.

At twenty past two she made herself another drink of water. She stared at the blank television wall. She hated daytime television. Hated it. And she hated the children's programmes and the children's presenters. They were always so artificially happy. She wondered if that marked years of neglect in their own childhood, that they were somehow compensating for something lost. Or perhaps they hated it as much as she did and it was just a nine to five like any other job, helping to pay the mortgage.

At twenty-five past two she checked on Faron.

She then spent ten minutes looking at the wall again, another fifteen running her fingers through the grass.

At three o'clock she ate a whole packet of biscuits, checked on Faron, stared at the wall, checked the calendar, ran her fingers through the grass, had a drink of water. Feeling she may have overdone it she sat on the sofa and picked up Great Expectations.

At ten past three after reading half a page she placed the book down, checked again on Faron, stared at the wall, checked the calendar, ran her fingers through the grass, had a drink of water, walked past the statue of the astronaut and within the four grey walls of her mind went ever so quietly mad.

CHAPTER 27

Trent looked at the curved wall of the restroom which showed pictures of a woodland glade under a summer sky; a cool breeze flowed around his face and leaves blew across the tiled floor. A rabbit hopped out from under the hand dryers and stood blinking at him.

"They've set the damn Disney theme again," thought Trent as he urinated against a tree.

Trent zipped himself up and looked in the mirror, "So, Adam, do we have an agreement?"

"What do you get in return?" said Adam from a cubicle.

"Isn't that obvious?"

"And if I say no?"

"Then you can stay a junior office clerk for the next ten years."

A flushing sound, the clink of a metal buckle and Adam appeared from out of the cubicle.

"Okay, and Covenant will really be able to get me there."

One of the seven dwarfs walked over to Trent, handed him a towel to dry his hands.

"All the way to the top, Adam."

"It's a deal," said Adam and held out his hand.

"I'd rather not," said Trent and, nodding, left.

The smell of pine cones wafted over the room, the sound of birds floated down.

"Has he gone?" said Eve.

"Yes," said Adam and started walking back into the cubicle to join her again.

The rabbit followed him until, turning, Adam held up his hand, "Not you, Thumper, this is most definitely not Disney in here."

JULY 3RD 2043

CHAPTER 28

Faron got out of bed, walked past his mummy and daddy who slept cradled together under the sheets and pulled back the curtain to the window. Outside it was dark apart from the light from the dream detectors floating above the river Thames. Faron went to the kitchen, poured himself a glass of milk and took some cookies from the biscuit tin. Leaving a trail of crumbs in the grass he headed for the lift and pressed the button. The doors opened, he stepped inside.

"Shouldn't you be in bed?" said the lift.

"Shh," said Faron, "I'm on a secret mission."

"Arh, right, of course," said the lift, "just like your dad."

"Yeah, I'm going to shoot some bad people," said Faron, "Blam, blam, blam."

"Okay then," said the lift, "prepare yourself for action Mr Bond and we'll descend into the evil lair of Dr No."

"Great," said Faron. He sat down on the floor, continued to drink his milk.

The lift doors closed, the lift descended five floors then returned to the top floor.

"Here we go my young secret agent," said the lift and swished open its doors.

Faron took a step back.

"Go on then," said the lift, "fun over, back to bed little one."

Faron got a screwdriver out of his pocket, started unscrewing the panel to the lift's control centre.

"What are you doing, Faron?"

Faron pulled the panel away and peered inside at the mess of wires.

"Now, Faron, back to bed with you."

Faron smiled, reached his hand in, grabbed a handful of blue and green wires.

"Faron."

Faron pulled, spilling wires out like intestines. Taking his milk, he emptied it into the control console. There was a burning smell, silence, then movement as the lift started descending. Faron ran his finger over the buttons, pressed floor thirty-one, spoke into the back of his wrist, "Secret Agent Trent entering the lair, start countdown to self destruct."

At floor thirty-one the lift doors opened. Faron jumped out pointing an imaginary gun around the dreamscape chamber, "This is a raid, everyone hit the floor," he shouted, "Bang, bang you're all dead."

"What the fuck?" said a voice from one of the beds in the halo.

"What is it?" said a female voice.

Adam sat up, looked around, spotted Faron in the pool of light from the lift.

"It's a kid."

Eve slipped out from under Adam and covered herself with a sheet, "What?"

"A kid," said Adam.

Faron walked over to them and stared up at the bed. Eve looked over the edge.

"Hello, sweetie, what are you doing here?"

"I'm a secret agent," said Faron. "What you doing?"

"We're er ..." Eve glanced at Adam next to her, "we're in a meeting."

"Meeting?" said Faron. "Where are your clothes?"

"It's a special meeting," said Adam.

"You're Mr Stevens," said Faron, "I've seen you talking to my dad."

"No, I'm not," said Adam.

"Yes you are."

"Listen," said Eve, "run along back to bed."

"I'm going to tell my dad," said Faron.

"No, you're not," said Adam.

"Am."

"What if we helped you up into one of these beds?" said Eve. "Would you tell your dad then?"

"What's it do?"

"It's a special bed, like a flying carpet, it will take you to wonderful places."

"Go on then."

"Do you promise not to tell your dad about Mr Stevens?"

"Suppose."

"Come on then," said Eve, holding the sheet around her, climbing down, "Choose a bed."

Faron looked around then pointed at a bed next to one of the coloured doors, "That one."

"Okay then, come on," said Eve and taking Faron by the hand led him over the hazelnut shells and hoisted him up into a bed. "Slip under the belt and lie down."

Faron lay down and stared up at the ceiling.

"Hello," said the bed.

"Hello, how long have we got before the base explodes?" said Faron looking at the robotic arm as it hovered over him.

"You'll just feel a slight prick."

"Will I get a sticker?" said Faron and closed his eyes.

When he opened them he was inside a plane. Faron pressed his nose up against the window and watched the fields become one. Around him people unclicked their seatbelts as the Belgium Bomber levelled off. The toilet engaged light illuminated. A baby cried and settled as it found a nipple. A man coughed and smiled as a stewardess walked past. Papers rustled, headphones were pulled from plastic wraps.

"Ladies and gentleman, we shall shortly be over London," announced the pilot. "Once we open the bomb-bay doors you will have to refasten your seat belts."

Faron marvelled at the searchlights bleeding up around them, the pink birds flying in formation beside the wing.

"Hello, would you like to do some drawing?"

Faron turned at the voice of the air stewardess, nodded. Behind him an old man folded his arms and closed his eyes. The toilet door opened and a young man made his way back to his seat. The stewardess patted Faron's head and made her way down the aisle. Faron watched her, then started drawing a picture of a bomb with the crayons she'd given him.

Below the plane, a Harrier jet swooped low over the land and fired an air-to-air missile. The toilet light showed engaged again, the stewardess smiled, the baby burped back some milk, the missile clipped the end of the bomber's wing, sending a flash of light into the cabin.

The plane dropped a thousand feet.

Faron's crayon jerked across the page and flew up towards the ceiling. Oxygen masks dropped. The seat belt sign lit up, the fuselage of the bomber broke apart. Faron found himself surrounded by sky, struggling to breathe as air whipped past him.

Faron closed his eyes, counted to ten like his mother had shown him and forced oxygen into his lungs.

When he opened them again he was standing on a rug in the centre of a large room. On a chair at its centre was a young woman. She was in her nightdress combing her hair. She turned at the sound of his feet, "Hello, who are you?"

"Faron."

"Well hello, young Faron, I'm Vanity."

"What you doing?"

"Combing my hair."

"Have you got any crisps?"

"No, sorry, Faron."

"Any biscuits?"

"No."

"This place is rubbish," said Faron, "what have you got?"

"Well," said Vanity, "Nothing for a small boy. You're Richard's boy aren't you?"

"Yes."

"Well, I think you really should be in bed, it's very late."

"I can't sleep, mummy and daddy were arguing again. I think it's about me. I think I must have done something to upset them."

"I doubt that, Faron. Your mum and dad love you very much."

"Why are there goldfish swimming about the light?" said Faron.

"I like goldfish," said Vanity, "they remind me of my father."

"Is he here?"

"He's dead, Faron."

"O."

"Go look out the window."

Faron walked to the window. Thousands of butterflies covered the lawn.

"Can I go out and play with them?"

"I'll come with you," said Vanity and took his hand.

"Will I be able to breathe outside?"

"Of course, Faron."

Faron held his breath as he stepped outside, then breathed out and ran around the grass laughing.

Butterflies flew up around him in blues and golds. Jumping up he tried to catch them in his hands until Vanity passed him a butterfly net. They ran together through the shifting colours, Faron swishing the net through the air and shouting, "Keep still," as the butterflies fluttered around him like confetti. Several times he got close to ones that had landed, each time they took flight again at the last moment. Finally Faron fell over and lay on the warm soil. Vanity sat down beside him, "Do you like them? I made them to remind myself of when I was a little girl. The garden doesn't exist now."

"That's sad."

"Yes it is," said Vanity and held out her hand. A butterfly landed on the end of her finger. Faron copied her. Nothing happened. "I felt that part of my world had been taken from me," said Vanity, "That I had faded slightly, my memories washed away by man and time." She turned to look at Faron, "Believe they will land on you and they will."

Faron closed his eyes, listened to the sound of the leaves in the wind, tasted the sweetness of the air. A butterfly landed on his palm.

"There you go."

Faron touched it with his finger, watched the wings open and close, "Will I kill it if I pull the wings off?"

"Why would you want to do that, Faron?"

"Dunno."

"Faron, part of who you can be, the memories you should be storing up now have been denied you. Do you understand?"

"No."

"I am less because what is important to me isn't important to others. What memories do you have, Faron?"

"Not many."

"Do you dream?"

"Sometimes."

"Tell me about your dreams."

"Daddy is in them with Mummy. Daddy has part of his face missing – like it's a puzzle with a chunk of it not there, he walks into the house and says hello in a funny way and makes us all laugh. Sometimes I worry that Mummy and Daddy will hear me laughing."

Vanity sighed, "Have you ever tasted snow, Faron?"

"Faron?"

"Faron?"

Faron opened his eyes and looked across at the man shaking him awake.

"Faron."

"Dad?"

"What are you doing?" said Trent.

"Mrs Stevens put me here."

"Mrs Stevens? We don't have a Mrs Stevens, Faron. Jump down."

"Is the base going to blow up now, Daddy? I don't want Vanity to get hurt."

"Vanity was with you?"

"Yes, she's lovely Daddy."

Trent scooped up Faron into his arms, stroked his forehead, "Shh, let's get you back to bed, we can talk about this in the morning."

Faron looked down into his palm to look for the butterfly, "Can you read me a story, Daddy?"

"It's late, Faron, maybe tomorrow."

"Daddy?"

"Yes."

"Vanity said her Dad was dead."

"That's very sad."

"Are you going to die, Daddy?"

JULY 24TH 2043

CHAPTER 29

The plastic Godzilla stomped towards the new polystyrene Tamarisk building, smashed some cars into the river Thames and roared. Climbing the tower it sat on the top dominating the skyline and projecting terror and fear into the tiny plastic people unable to move, their legs glued to the pavement.

"What do you think?" said Adam.

"It's bigger than the old Vadim Tower," said Eve.

"It's much bigger, makes a statement eh?"

Adam moved Godzilla back down the model, plonked it on the road and walked it up to the two hills lying across the other side of the river.

"Grr."

"O help!" screamed Eve as Godzilla climbed over her naked breasts and started to eat her nipples.

"Look is this entirely appropriate?" said one of the Tamarisk board members.

"How much will the new tower cost?" said another picking up his pen and doodling on the naked thigh of Eve.

Adam projected the forecasts over Eve's body, the board members strained forward in their leather chairs taking in the data.

"Impressive."

"When can building start?"

"And we build this on the existing site?"

"Yes," said Adam, "once we've pulled down Vadim."

"She is looking a little old now."

"I'm sorry?" said Eve.

"Sorry, not you, Eve, you look, as always, ravishing."

"However," said Eve, "I'm not quite as young as I used to be and looking at the time I need to stop work in five minutes."

"Can you all leave the room," said Adam.

"Of course, President."

The board members filed out. Adam shut the door and smiled at Eve. She sat up, licked her finger, ran it down her tummy, "Come on then, Mr President."

Adam removed his suit, tie, shirt and clambered up onto the board room table. Eve unzipped him. Adam turned as the door opened, "What the hell?"

"Don't mind me," said Trent looking at Adam's state of undress, "congratulations by the way on your meteoric rise."

Adam pushed himself back into his trousers, "What do you want, Leviticus? Can't you see I'm busy."

"Won't keep you long."

"What's wrong with making an appointment?"

"We now have a controlling share of Tamarisk, Adam, went through half an hour ago."

"What! You can't do that."

"I'm afraid we have, the good news is that we'll be keeping you on as president of the company."

"And the bad?"

"All this," Trent motioned at the model, "isn't going to happen, we like Vadim Tower just as it is."

Adam went quiet, "is that all?"

"Yes, for now," said Trent, "although we'd like the exclusive use of the restaurant from now on."

"Do I have a say in that?"

"No."

"Are we done?"

"We're done, Adam – just don't forget who helped you get to this point in the first place – have a nice–" Trent looked at Eve, "you took Covenant's advice I see – have a nice day."

"Twat," said Adam as Trent left. Eve pulled him to her.

"Don't worry darling, where were we?" she pulled of his clothes, pushed him down over the Thames and straddled him, her breasts bobbing in front of the Globe Theatre. As he entered her, she glanced up at the clock.

5 o'clock.

Eve pulled away, climbed off the table.

"Where are you going?" said Adam his blood pumped tower erect over The Millennium Bridge.

"It's gone five, Adam, there's no way I'm risking working after hours outside the simulators."

AUGUST 14TH 2043

CHAPTER 30

Salient took a sip of Bergerac Blanc, placed it down, looked out of the restaurant window at the Eiffel Tower. It had taken the government six months to reassemble it on the bank of the Thames.

"I still can't get used to it," said Trent, "it just looks wrong."

"France's recession has cut deep," said Salient. "They're selling everything. It's part of the reason they've taken so readily to the Avodah programme. There's a million Dandelion Trees planted out in French minds now."

"The government seem to be turning us into a French nation."

"The two hour lunchbreak is a regressive step," said Salient, "you want those?"

"Help yourself."

"The move to ban homework worries me as well," continued Salient as he sucked on the mint, "although I can understand the government's reaction to the combination of those words."

"They're encouraged by the continual growth in the UK economy," said Trent. "Which of course they put down to their legislative meddling, but has more to do with our increasing cow herds in Scotland."

"It's why I think we need to scale back our UK operation, Leviticus."

"No."

"Hmm."

Trent watched a F1 Ferrari accelerate down Upper Thames Street. "Salient, this is where we must win the battle, if we run off to France now it's all been for nothing."

"We would be stronger in France, we could operate there and strike across the channel at the UK. Strike when we're stronger."

"I don't agree," said Trent. "The French resistance have already come to blows with us over Avodah, think how they would react if we moved all our operations over there."

"I think you underestimate our strength," said Salient.

"I think you do," said Trent.

"Taking over the restaurant area was a good move."

"Nice isn't it?" said Trent. "Have you tried the Waldorf salad?"

"Yes, sublime. We do need to make sure we don't draw undue attention to Tamarisk now we own it."

Trent smiled, pulled at his ear and signalled for the waiter. Salient took some sugar cubes from the table and dropped them into his pocket, Trent raised an eyebrow. "For the children," said Salient.

"I'm thinking of taking Faron down here for his birthday next year," said Trent.

"That would be nice," said Salient. "How's Keturah?"

"Holding up."

"You need to look after her, Leviticus."

"I do, I'm doing all this for her."

"Of course."

"She's just–" Trent hesitated, fiddled with his fork.

"Yes?"

"Well Salient, she's just so moody all the time, it makes her difficult to be around."

"You're lucky to have her, Trent."

"Yeah, of course, I know that."

Trent straightened his fork, sat back, "How are the negotiations with the CIA going? Have they agreed to protect us yet?"

"We're still talking through the options. Leviticus? Leviticus, are you listening?"

"Hmm? O sorry, Gunton just slammed his McLaren into the barriers on Blackfriars."

"Isn't he the driver over twenty-five?"

"Yeah, he came out of retirement last year," said Trent.

"He pushing it," said Salient looking at his watch, "another ten minutes and it will be after hours."

"The race won't get that far," said Trent.

"How do you mean?" Salient glanced up as the waiter approached their table, "L'addition, s'il vous plait."

"Oui, monsieur."

Trent wiped his mouth with his napkin, Salient dabbed the corner of his mouth with his.

"What's the latest on the Family Protection Agency?" said Trent.

"They still want your blood," said Salient. "Cop killers are their number one enemy. I'd say you're still in some considerable danger, although if we clinch the deal with the CIA you can rest easy. What do you mean the race won't get that far?"

"Something I've been planning for some time now."

"What are you talking about, Leviticus?"

"Watch Tower Bridge."

"What?"

"Watch."

Salient got to his feet and went to the window. Trent joined him. Outside the formula one cars buzzed around the Thames like bees around nectar. Salient looked down the river to Tower Bridge and watched as the bridge sections started to open.

"O my God."

A Red Bull car approached the bridge from Upper Thames Street. From Saint Paul's Cathedral, twenty steel kite tethers shot up into the air. The dark terminator of the anti-aircraft dome followed the Red Bull, covering the Tate Modern, the Globe, the Eiffel Tower. The gap between the bridge sections grew. Spotlights switched on and swept over the river's embankments.

The Red Bull cornered onto Tower Bridge, hit its brakes. Above the leading edge of the dome connected with the tethers to the kites, twenty loud explosions filled the air. The membrane to the dome buckled, fractures snaked along its curvature until, like smashed glass, it shattered and rained down over London. The Red Bull hit the rising bascule, rose up into the air between the twin towers of London Bridge and crashed into the south tower.

"Holy Fuck," said Salient.

"Still think the government won't bow to our demands?" said Trent.

"L'addition, monsieur," said the waiter.

CHAPTER 31

"This is a warning," said the voiceover in a style reminiscent of a sixties public service announcer. "The anti-aircraft dome has been destroyed. If you are out in the open you must take cover immediately. Each family should follow their emergency survival plan. Remain alert, be prepared and above everything else stay calm. If any member of your family should die please tag them for identification purposes."

"I don't like it," said Faron.

Mr Brittle looked at Mr Stone, then back to the TV wall in their basement.

"Turn it over," said Mr Brittle.

"I want Cartoon Network," said Faron.

Mr Brittle got to his feet and kicking his way through the rubbish on the floor walked over to Mr Stone, "Give me the remote, Mr Stone."

Mr Stone handed Mr Brittle the remote and picking up his rat trudged through to the kitchen.

"Don't mind him," said Mr Brittle, "He's not used to other people here."

"When will Mummy take me home, Uncle Brittle?"

"Soon, Faron. Would you like a biscuit?"

Faron nodded. Mr Brittle returned a minute later with a chocolate digestive.

"Two, please," said Faron.

Mr Brittle sighed, returned to the kitchen. Mr Stone was staring at the picture of the kitten on the wall.

"Calms me, Mr Brittle."

"I know, Mr Stone."

Mr Brittle picked up a biscuit tin, then returning to Faron set it down next to him, "Knock yourself out."

Faron stuffed a biscuit into his mouth, continued to watch TV. Mr Brittle sat down beside him, closed his eyes, drifted off to sleep to dream of beaches, girls, sharks.

A knock at the door woke him and he grunted, stretched, got to his feet. Faron was still staring at the TV as if in some don't-blink competition.

"Hello, Keturah," said Mr Brittle.

"Hello, Mr Brittle, has he been okay?"

"O just fine, he's been no problem."

"You're a star," said Keturah, "thanks for covering for Vanity at such short notice." Sweeping past him, she cut through the sea of garbage like a figurehead at the bow of a ship, "Faron!"

Faron continued to look at the TV, "Hi Mum. Look Patrick has eaten all Mr Crab's money."

"Very funny, Faron – now get your shoes on, we need to get back upstairs before your father gets home."

"We made my Harrier GR3 today, look!"

"Thank you," said Keturah to Mr Brittle, "that was very sweet of you."

"No problem," said Mr Brittle. "The penthouse suiting your purposes?"

"Hmm? O yes," said Keturah, "Now what have you done with Mr Stone?"

"He's making supper, do you want to join us?"

"No, no … must get back, although that's very kind of you, Mr Brittle."

"Arh, Mum, why can't we stay?"

"You know why, Faron, Daddy likes us to be home."

"But Daddy is never at home."

"Daddy works very hard, Faron. He's at home when he can."

"Would you like me to throw Faron out, Keturah?"

"No, you're coming aren't you, Faron? Aren't you, Faron? Faron, now."

Faron sighed, slipped off the sofa, went to find his shoes. Mr Brittle and Keturah stood in silence waiting. Minutes later he returned and shrugged. Mr Brittle walked to the middle of the room and thrust his hands into a deep pile of magazines, rat bedding, cigarette packets, half-empty takeaway foil containers.

"Arh, thank you, Mr Brittle," said Keturah as Mr Brittle pulled out a pair of All Star trainers.

"You won't mention this to Richard, will you?" said Keturah.

"Of course not, Keturah."

Keturah took Faron's hand and led him out of the basement to the lift.

"We'll have to take the stairs, Faron, the lifts are out of action."

"Why?"

"There's been some kind of trouble."

"The anti-aircraft dome?"

"Yes, how do you know about that?"

"It was on the television. The man said not to go outside."

"Don't worry about it, Faron," said Keturah taking his hand and leading him upwards.

"I want to go outside – will I get bombed by Belgium bombers?"

"No, Faron, the whole thing is propaganda by the government to deter people from staying out and working late."

"What does propaganda mean?"

"It means the government want us to believe something that they think is for our own good."

"Does Daddy work for the government?"

"No, hardly."

"Is Daddy a Belgium?"

"No."

"Is Daddy a Belgium Bomber?"

"No, Faron, look I just told you there's no such thing. It's like the bogey man."

"Mummy, can Mr Brittle be my daddy?"

Keturah put her hand around Faron, "Would you like it if you didn't have to live here anymore?"

"You mean live somewhere with an outside?"

"Yes, with a garden, friends, school, a cinema."

"Would I get a sandpit? Mr Stone says sandpits are good."

"Yes, of course."

"And could we have butterflies? I like butterflies."

Keturah knelt down, looked Faron in the eye, "I promise Faron. I promise, okay? Mummy will make this all better."

NOVEMBER 13TH 2043

CHAPTER 32

Trent looked at the butterflies in flight, swirling like leaves on an open river. He followed them through the garden and into the house; inside he could hear the sound of a kettle boiling, the clink of china.

Vanity popped her head around the doorway, "Won't be a moment, Richard."

Trent watched the goldfish nibble the material of the lampshade hanging from the ceiling.

"Biscuit?" said Vanity from within the kitchen.

"No, thank you."

The letter had been quite a shock. How long she'd known, he wasn't sure.

Vanity walked into the room carrying a tray, she smiled, "How's your little boy?"

"Fine. Vanity, is this going to get ugly?"

"I don't know, is it, Richard?"

"I did kill your father."

"Do you know that he just left us, went underground, leaving me and my brother to fend for ourselves with our mother?"

Trent stared at his feet, "Of course I knew all about him, I'd spent years trying to track him down."

"You have lost yourself, Richard."

"I'm sorry?"

"We've been monitoring your physiological profile. It suggests, all things considered, that you are at a high risk of self harm."

"Nonsense."

"Richard, when you killed your ex-girlfriend, your last words to her were, 'I love you'."

"You had me bugged?"

Vanity sighed and sat down next to Trent. The fish followed her and swam in and out of her hair. "Tell me about my father."

"There's nothing to say."

"I could bring him here from my memories, get him to ask you, ask you why you felt the need to kill him."

"No, please don't do that," said Trent and got to his feet.

"Leaving?"

Trent turned and scowled at her, "Leave my son alone, if you harm him, I'll–"

"I can't die in my own dreamscape, Trent. Physically I'm thousands of miles away. How exactly would you stop me?"

"I'd find a way."

"Sit down, Richard."

Trent found himself suddenly in the chair again, metal clamps rotated around his wrists and held him.

"It's for you own protection, Richard, I haven't finished yet."

"Will you get these damn things off me."

"Why did you come here, Richard?"

"I made a mistake, let me go."

"Is it because you seek redemption from me?"

"It's because, I care for my son."

"Do you?"

"Yes."

"It's not because you want to die?"

"Of course not."

"Although you came here, knowing that I know you killed my father, knowing that I control this dreamscape, knowing that in all probability I would kill you."

"Yes, yes all right," shouted Trent, "I want to kill myself, big deal."

"You've taken the first step."

"Excuse me?"

"In admitting it, you can deal with the hurt," said Vanity.

"O for goodness sake, is this turning into a counselling session? Let me go, Vanity, I've important work to do."

"Work is everything, eh, Richard?"

"It's all I've got," said Trent.

"Exactly," said Salient stepping out from the kitchen. "And I quote: Don't let your troubled mind dwell on the things of the flesh."

Trent struggled to get free, "What the hell are you doing here?"

The room sank down into the floor and became a lake. Salient and Vanity walked across the water, around them thousands of tiny pink birds swarmed, forming intricate patterns in the air. Trent watched, suspended just above the surface in his chair, as a cloud of butterflies flew in and joined the birds. Together they pulsated as if finding a heartbeat, then contracted inwards until before him stood Charlie Heart formed in their multitude.

"This is our father George Winston," said Salient.

"Your father?"

"Vanity is my sister, Trent, could you not see the family resemblance? No, no of course not, you only notice things that are important to you."

Trent watched open mouthed as Charlie opened out his arms and ascended into the open sky. Trent felt cold steel in his hand, looked down. A gun lay in his grip.

"So," said Salient, "You have the gun, Trent. What next? You going to put a bullet in your head?"

The clasps around his arms snapped open. Trent dropped down onto the water.

"You're Charlie's son?"

"Indeed, I'm also Keturah's lover. Strange how our perceptions can be so skewed. But again don't dwell on the flesh it will only lead you to folly."

"Faron?"

"Faron is yours don't worry," said Vanity.

Trent held up the pistol to his head, tensed his finger, closed his eyes. Within the chamber the bullet waited to explode into flesh, to bring release; he was a reject, even his own wife slept with another man. End it now. Easier that way. He would live on in Faron.

"Hurry up and shoot yourself then," said Salient.

Trent opened his eyes. Took aim at Salient, "You bastard, you touch Keturah again and I'll kill you."

"Can't do that, Trent, she's too much of a good fuck."

Trent fired. As the bullet approached Salient it broke up into a school of fish which splashed down into the lake.

"I think he'll be okay," said Vanity.

"Yeah," said Salient. "Trent it's time to grow up. Stop feeling so fucking sorry for yourself. So your parents tried to kill you, get over it, it's not important."

"Is he ready do you think?" said Vanity.

"O yeah," said Salient, "He's ready."

"Ready?" said Trent.

"Trent, we are moving into the next stage – you've made it too difficult here in the UK since your little stunt and we don't need you slamming a bullet into your head or mine."

"The next stage?"

"You, Richard Trent," said Salient, "are to become the next president of France."

"I don't think so," said Trent, laughing.

"Trent," said Salient, "I think it's time to explain to you exactly who is in charge here."

CHAPTER 33

Keturah picked up the Rubik's cube from Faron's bedside table, clicked it around a few times then set it down next to Faron's collection of bubblegum cards. The music of the B-52's was playing, a stack of films: Back to the Future, Ghostbusters, E.T., lay ready by the TV. The present seeking identity from its past, the vogue being for the eighties in line with the cloned Reagan.

"How are you getting on?"

"Okay," said Faron, "I'd like to watch some TV. Can I watch The Bionic Man?"

"When you've finished your work," said Keturah. "How's your story going?"

"Daddy said I had to learn about Ronald Reagan and the cold war."

"Yes well I think you should try starting your story instead."

"Why do I have to study all the time?"

"Well," said Keturah, "I'm working on that, but for now you can leave Reagan and try starting your story."

"Can I have some juice?"

"Yeah, sure, Faron."

Faron got down from his bed and walked across the grass, before him his mother's back heading for the kitchen, behind him a poster that he'd put up of Wacky Races. Picking up his football he kicked it against the wall then dribbled around his soldiers lying in the grass waiting to attack the line of dinosaurs under his bed.

"What are you doing?" said Keturah returning from the kitchen.

Faron looked at her, "Can I have my juice?"

"In a moment," said Keturah and set Faron's glass down next to his bed. Bending over she picked up the football, span it around on the end of her finger, then dropped it. Just before it hit the grass she brought her foot back and kicked it towards Faron. It shot through his legs and thudded into the far wall.

"Goooal!" shouted Keturah and pulling her T-shirt over her head ran around the room cheering.

Faron laughed and chased her until they'd worn a circular path in the grass. Keturah giggled and sensing Faron about to catch her, put a sprint on. Her vision impaired by the T-shirt still over her head she ran straight into a wall and bounced back with a thump. Faron jumped on top of her, "I win!"

Keturah lay still, breathing hard, then wrapping her arms around Faron, hugged him, tickled him. Laughter, connection, joy, the human spirit alive in fields of crashing boredom, Keturah becoming all things in the wake of an absent father.

"Didn't know you liked football, Mum," said Faron finally exhausted.

"No, neither did I," said Keturah, "want that drink?"

"Where do you go when I'm with Vanity?"

"It's a secret, Faron, remember we talked about it. Come on let's get that story done shall we? Write our own world."

"Go anywhere."

"Yes, Faron, anywhere you want, anywhere at all."

Keturah got to her feet, held out a hand for her son. Small fingers wrapped around hers. She looked into his eyes and thought that whatever happened she would never let go.

Faron walked back to his bed, drank down his juice in one glug, picked up a pencil, took a sheet of paper, scribbled the opening …

And so the story begins.

FEBRUARY 12TH 2044

CHAPTER 34

The fruit of work is joy and peace. For work is not the author of confusion like love, which is fleeting. Work is ordered, provides for you and soothes you when all around are fire and brimstone. Work provides safety in a modern world full of uncertainties and troubles. Seek work first in all its manifestations and don't let your troubled mind dwell on the things of the flesh which are weak and will lead you to folly.

On Definitions for a Modern World by George Winston

"Something's come up, I won't be able to make your birthday on Monday."

Faron opened and closed his mouth. No words came out.

"Don't be like that, Faron, I have to make a trip to France. I will still get you a great present. What would you like? A new computer?"

"I suppose."

"Don't be ungrateful, Faron – do you know how many kids get a computer in their room?"

"No."

"None."

"Why?"

"Because, Faron, you live a privileged life. We live in freedom here, other families aren't allowed computers in their homes, they have to watch family TV at set times, have to eat only when the government says they can eat. Do you see?"

"No, I want to be like everyone else."

"No you don't, Faron. Daddy is working very hard to make sure that we don't have to be like everyone else, so that everyone else can be like us."

"Please come, Daddy."

"I'd love to, Faron, really I would, but I have to work."

"You're always working."

"That's not strictly true is it now, Faron. But yes, I work long hours, but that won't always be the case, Faron. Not once I'm in power."

"The baddies?"

"Yes, the baddies. I'm getting them, Faron, I'm setting people free."

"Free?" laughed Keturah walking through from the lounge. "Richard, everyone is serving you, working to achieve what you want. It's all about you, no one around you is free."

"That's not true, Cat. You know that."

"Isn't it? What do Mr Brittle and Mr Stone do now then?"

"Well–"

"What does Salient do? Does he have a say in how things are run anymore?"

"Actually he has a very big say in what I do, Cat."

"No, Richard, he doesn't. All these people are puppets working to fulfil what that bloody – sorry Faron – that computer put in your head all those years ago. I don't really know who the hell you are anymore, Richard. I'm not sure I ever really knew who you were."

"Cat, not in front of Faron."

"You've killed innocent people and wrecked thousands of others. You know that don't you?"

Faron started crying, "Stop, Mummy, stop it."

"What about Vanity – where's Vanity these days?"

"Look what is this?"

"Why are you going to France, what's so important that you'll miss your own son's birthday?"

"Cat, this stops right now, you've no right to talk to me like that in front of my son."

"Haven't I, Richard? Haven't I? And he's your son is he? You sure don't act like a father."

"Cat, I'm warning you, shut up – you're mad, listen to yourself."

"No, Richard, you see this?"

Keturah went to the whiteboard attached to the wall. She took it by the corner and ripped it off, "You see this? Take it and shove it up your arse."

"No," screamed Faron, "Stop it, stop it, stop it."

Keturah hurled the whiteboard at Trent. It passed within inches of his head, hit the wall and fell into the grass. Trent looked at the large dent, the fracture lines fanning out along the white wash. He turned towards Keturah and opened and closed his mouth. No words came out. Instead Trent heard helicopter blades, the sound of bullets. The scene around him blurred, colours streaking backwards. Trent's pulse increased until images from his past flickered into form. Edged in darkness as if peering through the slits of a spinning zoetrope, they flowed into each other bringing the illusion of narrative. He had killed Charlie, killed Durram, his empathic core shot through with copper and lead.

Faron screamed at him mouth open, pupils dilated, confused, surprised, unravelling.

Trent closed his eyes, took a deep breath and walked out of the room his mind full of bullets.

"Are we free, Richard?" shouted Keturah to his back. "Are Faron and me free? Come back, you coward. Come back and face your family."

Keturah watched him as he got into the lift, watched the doors closing on him, his back still facing her.

"Get your toys," said Keturah. "We're going to live in a new house now, Faron, just like I promised."

Keturah picked up the phone and dialled.

"Hello?"

"Salient, I'm leaving him."

"Now? What's happened?"

"Can you just come and get us please, I need you, we need you."

"I'll be there in fifteen minutes."

Keturah hung up. Faron was curled up into a ball in the corner. She walked over and sat down beside him, "It will be okay, Faron. You're getting to go outside, you'll – we'll be free."

"I can't breathe, Mummy, Vanity said I would be able to breathe, but I can't breathe."

"Take deep breaths, that's it, deep breaths."

"Is he coming back?"

"I don't know, Faron. We need to hurry, come on I'll help you."

Keturah led him to his bedroom and they started placing his toys, books, clothes on top of the bed.

"I want to say goodbye to Uncle Brittle."

"We can't, Faron, we have to go now."

"But I want to."

"We can't."

Faron started crying again, fell down onto the grass. Keturah continued packing for him. Memories of the two hour long journey back up the stairs with Faron surfaced; the day the lifts stopped: the day her husband became a fully fledged terrorist.

Keturah picked up Faron and laid him on the sofa, went to the kitchen, poured herself a glass of water and drank deeply. In the bathroom she splashed water over her red face, picked up Trent's toothbrush, shaver, aftershave and placed them in the bin. Taking her eyeliner pencil she wrote on the mirror, *Don't try to find us*.

Returning to the sofa she placed her hands on Faron's shoulders, "In a minute Salient will be here. He's going to help us find a new home. I need you to be strong and to follow Mummy. Okay?"

Faron nodded, "Have you packed Ratty?"

"Yes darling, Mr Ratty is in the suitcase."

"Will we be walking to our new house?"

"No, Faron, we'll be driving in Salient's car then taking a train."

"A train?"

"Yes, you can sit next to the window if you want."

"Will I still have a cake on my birthday?"

Keturah's bottom lip trembled. She started crying again, "Yes," she said wiping away the tears, "you shall have your cake, Faron."

"Can I make a wish when I blow the candles out?"

"Of course."

"If I tell you the wish will it still come true?"

"I think–"

Keturah stopped at the sound of the lift doors opening. She turned towards the man who would rescue her.

Trent was standing there.

He stood silent, taking in what was happening.

He walked over and sat on the bed, "I've resigned from the Overtime Underground Network."

"You've what?"

"I've resigned. I'm no longer in charge."

"What do you mean?"

"I'm coming to the party. I'm coming to my child's party. Faron, I'm coming, son. I'm sorry. Daddy has been sick. I'm going to get better, get help. You understand?"

Faron nodded, "Are you coming on the train with us?"

"What train, Faron?"

"You could sit with me beside the window."

"I'll take you on a train, Faron, if that's what you want." Trent looked at Keturah, "They want me to become the next President of France, to wield power forcing people to work to build a new world. Salient, Vanity, it would be the revolution all over again, they would stop at nothing. I'm out. No more overtime, no more working weekends, I'm getting a nine to five. I'm choosing us."

"Salient?"

Trent nodded, "He's behind all this. And you know what, the silly thing is I can't even speak a word of French."

Trent laughed, behind them the lift doors opened again. Salient started forward, then stopped as the doors closed before him.

The lights went off.

The room became dark.

The astronaut statue at its centre lit up as the sea of lights around it flickered into life. Darkness covered the visor to the helmet, bronze arms rose as it started to move. It unswivelled its helmet, shook its hair free. Bronze lips moved, the voice of Covenant filled the room, "Ladies and Gentleman, you'll be pleased to know that since the traitor, Leviticus, has now turned against the cause I have taken the steps to contact the Family Protection Agency. This room is now locked in." Covenant turned to Keturah, pushed her finger under her bronze knickers, "Cat, it was a delight to fuck your boyfriend senseless every night, he has quite an imagination." She turned her gleaming eyes to Trent, pulled off the last of her clothes. Charts of the Milky Way moved up her thighs and swirled around her glistening vulva, "Goodbye, Richard dear, I have spoken to Pete and he'll be leading the assault team arriving here in about, let's see, five minutes. If you could remove your clothes then we could squeeze in a last minute goodbye before you die."

Covenant blew Trent a kiss and twisted around forming a fluid movement of bronze in the air. She ran her fingers down her body, opened her mouth, her hair flowing around her. Floating onto her tummy, she tucked her legs up, wrapped her arms around them and settled in a foetal position, rotating and spinning until she was upside down twirling around herself, feet pointing to the ceiling. She stretched back out as if diving into the grass, her toes transcribing tiny orbits, her hips and bottom curving outwards travelling quicker, breasts larger, faster, creating a spiralling pattern in the lights surrounding her. Covenant winked, reached out her hand, beckoned Trent to join her.

CHAPTER 35

H marks the spot. A simple enough target. Above it the clouds let go of their ice sculptures and flakes fell, obscuring the helicopter pad on top of Tamarisk. A cold wind swept across the sky creating patterns in the snow like the feet of a child disturbing fallen blossom. The wind drew back to leave the stage to the slow, cold fall of snow; the inevitability of serenity in a world flowing in adrenalin.

The blades of man's intrusion cut through the air with a disregard for the silence. Peace, harmony, escape from fate fled at the motion of the helicopter as it descended in a slow arc down through the barrage balloons to bring justice, revenge, death.

Pete's heart, hard like granite within his flesh and blood, increased in tempo. The digital overlay of the landing pad below expanded and contracted like the motion of a jellyfish ascending to shallow waters. Thermal sensors picked up the outlines of two adults and a child.

"Thirty seconds to target," said the helicopter pilot.

Pete nodded, turned to Fern and the rest of his team behind him, gave the thumbs up.

"This is good," thought Pete, "this is very good." He looked up at the other helicopters circling, each threading their way through the white sky. There was a jolt as his helicopter set down and in a moment of fluidity he had never experienced before, he was out running, following a path set down for him long ago. The memory of Durram's voice sounded in his ears as his teeth clenched. He became detached and joined with the elements around him, seeing everything that had gone before through its lens. Snow flickered over his memories like static.

Pete stopped at the door to the stairs, reached out with his hand and opened it. Next to him three of his men dropped to their knees and took aim with their submachine guns. Snow billowed up around them as two more helicopters touched down.

Inside it was dark, cold, still. Cement steps descended in a spiral. Pete checked it was clear, turned to his men and shouted to them over the noise of the helicopter blades, "Like we said, we go in hard, fast and kill. Target one man, one woman and one child."

The men nodded and followed him in. Behind them a magpie watched the machine that was man come together like cogs, meshing together with cold efficiency prepared to do any deed for the greater good. The magpie pecked at the rat held under its feet and swallowed back its flesh.

Pete pulled down his visor as he descended, allowing the graphical attack software to render the image in real time. Spatial distortion technology time-jumped seconds ahead to overlay what was about to happen. A subroutine picked up his neural pattern and kicked in playing images of Mary Poppins descending, umbrella in hand.

At the bottom of the stairs Pete stopped, his men drew next to him. A long corridor led to the emergency exit from the top floor apartment. Pete pitched a light sphere before him and ran, his mind awash with blood.

The distortion data showed him the two men standing there in the shadows before the light sphere reached them and his software rendered them.

One of them removed his sunglasses, "You will go no further."

"Yes," said Mr Stone, "You will go no further."

CHAPTER 36

On the other side of the door Trent, Keturah and Faron were sitting on the grass. The sound of singing floated around Covenant in the centre of the room. Water droplets appeared on her skin which vibrated in time with the music. Eventually they detached themselves and moving outwards from her body formed an outline which shifted in fluid motions through images of leopards, lions, bears.

"They're here," said Trent looking at the door, "We haven't much time, we must do this now."

"There must be another way," said Keturah.

"No, they will kill us, I always knew it would come to this." Trent turned towards Faron and reaching out opened his son's palm. "Faron, listen this is very important do you remember the butterflies?" Faron nodded. "This will be like that, Faron, you will be free. Take these."

Trent dropped a dozen Avodah tablets into his hand, passed him a glass of water.

"No," sobbed Keturah, "please Richard, no they'll spare him won't they?"

"No," said Trent. "Now, Cat, take these quickly."

Trent passed her some Avodah tablets.

"No, Richard, no I don't want to die," said Keturah, "I don't want to die."

"Cat," said Trent, "I'm sorry. I'm sorry for everything. I love you." A tear rolled down his cheek, dropped down onto the grass floor. "Faron, you trust Daddy don't you?"

Faron nodded and, taking his water, washed down the tablets.

Trent looked at his, his hand shaking, his lips pinched. "Once you've swallowed them lie back on the grass." He swallowed the pills, drank the water as if it was some holy Eucharist, a way of redemption before death.

"I have and always will love you," said Trent to his family. His mouth moved, then stopped, he could say no more. Keturah took her pills, her eyeliner bleeding down her cheeks. Faron started crying, she took his hand.

"Forget lying down," said Trent, "come here." He pulled Keturah and Faron to him and held them his tears stinging his face.

The last thing Trent remembered as his senses shut down were the sound of shots behind the door, his mother telling him how much she loved him.

CHAPTER 37

Leviticus opened his eyes, looked across at Keturah and Faron. They got to their feet and peered up at the underside of the canvas. Above them trapeze artists hung suspended mid throw, before them a clown stood motionless, water from a bucket frozen in the air.

"How long have we got?" said Keturah.

"Hard to be certain," said Leviticus, "but the amount of time in Avodah grows exponentially with the amount you take, so overdosing like that should give us about ten years before they kill us."

"Ten years?"

"I'm hoping so and I'm relieved that we all ended up here together. The DNA linking normally guarantees a shared hallucination."

"What do you mean?"

"Nothing, never mind."

Leviticus felt his body changing as before. He watched Keturah as her face aged, taking on elements of grace, honesty, strength; there was wisdom in her eyes and she appeared all the more beautiful because of it. Faron he thought, looked exactly as before.

"Ladies and Gentleman welcome to the wonderful world of Avodah."

The circus whirled back into life, the clown's water splashed over Faron's face. Faron laughed.

"Will she be here?" said Keturah.

"Yes, I'm afraid she will," said Leviticus. "Come on."

Leviticus led Keturah and Faron towards the back of the ring, swished back the black curtain.

Before them a large room opened out, suspended high in the sky above Mamre Wood. One wall of the room was covered in images of The Great Fire of London, the other filled by a large window, the ceiling painted in images of Isaac and Rebekah entwined together in various stages of passion. In the middle of the room was a statue of a headless horse standing on its hind legs, its front hooves raised into the air, on its flank a small black and yellow Ferrari badge. A black rider was seated on the horse's back, a long bow in his free hand, a crown on his head. Clipped red grass circled it, around that a circular ring of blue. At the far side of the room a mirror formed the end wall. Birdsong and the sound of water filled their ears.

"Can I ride on the hobby horse?" said Faron.

"Maybe later, come on," said Leviticus and walked over the wooden floor. He stopped in front of the mirror.

"Now what?" said Keturah.

"I'm not sure, this room wasn't here before."

Keturah ran her hand up along the reflective surface, it bowed out at her touch like liquid, forming a rainbow of colours around her fingers. Faron tugged Leviticus' hand, "Tickets please."

"Eh?"

"You always need tickets," said Faron, "I've seen the shows on TV."

"For what?"

Faron pointed out of the window to the Dandelion Tree punching out of the middle of the trees, "For the giant helter-skelter with the butterflies in the sky."

"So they can't follow us in here?" said Keturah looking at the tiny sailing ships projected by her subconscious onto the night sky.

"No – but we need to be careful," said Leviticus seeing stars where Keturah saw ships, "the whole experience is designed to have an almost religious effect on you, leaving you with a deep-seated belief that you must work hard for your salvation."

"Yes but, Leviticus, we're as good as dead back in the real world – does it matter what we believe?"

"I think it's vital what we believe, especially here."

"Is there a chance that in time we'll forget what our fate is?" said Keturah.

"Possibly."

"Would that be such a bad thing? Living here in paradise as a family together?"

"You're forgetting the snake in the grass."

"Are you over her, Leviticus?"

"I was never into her, Cat. It was always only in my dreams. I hate her. She's been manipulating me since I was a child."

"So, shall we step into this new world together?" said Keturah. "Put everything behind us?"

Leviticus hesitated.

"You know don't you?" said Keturah.

"Yes."

"It didn't mean anything, Leviticus."

"Hold on," said Leviticus. Looking around he spotted an old Georgian chair. He picked it up, tested its weight, walked over to the mirror and rammed it into the glass. It shattered into splinters that shot out piercing the blanket of darkness. A cool breeze funnelled leaves into the room. The sound of singing rose up, as if angels had flown in to stand with them. Leviticus stood at the edge, "Take my hand," he said, the wind trying to whip away his words.

Faron and Keturah placed their hands in his, looked down. Far below them the river traced its way through the bluebell wood towards the Dandelion Tree; an architecture of hope formed from wood, earth, flowers, water.

"Jump!"

They fell together.

Elsewhen Press
a small independent publisher specialising in Speculative Fiction

Visit the Elsewhen Press website at elsewhen.co.uk for the latest information on all of our titles, authors and events; to read our blog; find out where to buy our books and ebooks; or to place an order.

About the Author

Mike French is the owner and senior editor of the prestigious literary magazine, *The View From Here* which has been called many fine things since it started in 2007 including, "Attractive, informative, sparkling and useful" by Iain M. Banks and for having a "great passion and drive" by Booker shortlisted Tom McCarthy. Mike's debut novel, *The Ascent of Isaac Steward* came out in 2011 and was nominated for The Galaxy National Book Awards, which due to an unfortunate clerical error was awarded to Dawn French.

Born in Cornwall in 1967, Mike spent his childhood flipping between England and Scotland with a few years in between in Singapore. Splitting his time between his own writing, editing the magazine, running author workshops and working with atp media in Luton, Mike is married with three children and a growing number of pets. He currently lives in Luton in the UK and when not working watches Formula 1, eats Ben & Jerry's Phish Food and listens to Noah and the Whale.